IN EARLY JUNE 1964,

the Benevolent Home for Necessitous Girls burns to the ground, and its vulnerable residents are thrust out into the world. The orphans, who know no other home, find their lives changed in an instant. Arrangements are made for the youngest residents, but the seven oldest girls are sent on their way with little more than a clue or two to their pasts and the hope of learning about the families they have never known. On their own for the first time in their lives, they are about to experience the world in ways they never imagined...

Shattered Glass

TERESA TOTEN

ORCA BOOK PUBLISHERS

Library and Archives Canada Cataloguing in Publication

Toten, Teresa, 1955–, author
Shattered glass / Teresa Toten.
(Secrets)

Issued in print, electronic and audio disc formats.
ISBN 978-1-4598-0671-9 (pbk.).—ISBN 978-1-4598-0672-6 (pdf).—
ISBN 978-1-4598-0673-3 (epub).—ISBN 978-1-4598-1096-9 (audio disc)

I. Title. II. Series: Secrets (Victoria, B.C.)
PS8589.O6759S53 2015   jc813'.54   C2015-901741-6
C2015-901742-4   C2015-901743-2

First published in the United States, 2015
Library of Congress Control Number: 2015935522

Summary: In this YA novel, Toni travels to Toronto to unearth the truth about the mother she believes hurt and then abandoned her.

Orca Book Publishers is dedicated to preserving the environment and has printed this book on Forest Stewardship Council® certified paper.

Orca Book Publishers gratefully acknowledges the support for its publishing programs provided by the following agencies: the Government of Canada through the Canada Book Fund and the Canada Council for the Arts, and the Province of British Columbia through the BC Arts Council and the Book Publishing Tax Credit.

Cover design by Teresa Bubela
Front cover image by iStockphoto.com; back cover images by Shutterstock.com
Author photo by Matthew Wiley

ORCA BOOK PUBLISHERS
www.orcabook.com

Printed and bound in Canada.

18 17 16 15 • 4 3 2 1

In memory of Jack and Mary Toten

"Twist and Shout"

(THE BEATLES)

FIRE!!!

It was the fire dream again, always the same dream. But this time it was different. This time, despite the fear that was as worn and familiar as a threadbare shirt, I knew that I had to save Betty. Then I was washed in shame. How did shame sneak into my dream? We were seven, had always been "the Seven." I had to save them all! But mainly I had to save Betty. It'd been like that since the beginning. Ever since I got there when I was three. Betty needed nonstop saving because she was too innocent, too trusting. I was not, because of my past, the things I almost remembered. My dreams were my memory. I had no proof, but there were things I knew.

It had been almost thirteen years of trying to save Betty and almost thirteen years of fire dreams.

But this was the first time that Betty had been in the dream.

Smoke slid down the back of my throat and crawled back up again. I could taste it.

That was weird.

"Betty!" I screamed at the shape in the bed beside me. "Betty, wake up!" The words got caught in the smoke and tripped over themselves. "Betty—fire, fire!"

She woke up and hit me. No. Wait. It was me who woke up from deep in the bowels of the dream. But Betty had definitely hit me. "What the…Betty, why did you…?"

"Can't you smell it? What's the matter with you?" She did not apologize for hitting me. "Wake up, Toni! Toni, get up!"

"Huh?"

"There's a fire!" she screamed. "Something is on fire!"

Then I saw it. Hungry wisps sneaking under the door. Just like the other times, in my dreams and before my dreams.

Before this place.

She shook me hard. There was a taste of ashes in my mouth that soaked up all the spit. That was the way the dream always started, with the taste of ashes. I couldn't swallow, but I could taste the fire.

"Toni, there's a fire, I can smell it! Toni, are you awake?"

"Yes, yeah!" I croaked. "There's smoke!" It slithered lazily into our room.

Jumpin' Joe screamed from somewhere downstairs. "Fire! Fire! Fire!"

It was real.

Joe, our cook and my boss, for sure had never been in my dreams. Betty tried to turn on the light. She kept flicking the switch on and off, on and off. "Stop!" I yelled. I grabbed for her arm, missed and got a handful of nightgown instead. "We've got to go, got to get out!"

"Get Cady, get Malou, make sure they're up," she screamed.

I checked the door, which wasn't hot, but it opened to a wall of smoke. I froze. Joe was still yelling. "Joe?" We couldn't see him. He called up to us from somewhere below.

"Toni? You girls get the rest of the Seven. I'm gonna get the Littles." The Little Ones. There were seventeen of them.

I got pushed. Betty? She turned left and I turned right. I ran barefoot into the smoke, trying not to eat it, and pounded on a door, screaming my head off with a mouth full of soot. I wasn't even sure whose door it was. The smoke had made me stupid. "Sara! Malou! Cady! Dot!" Betty was pounding and screaming too. The same names over and over again. "Dot! Cady! Malou! Sara!"

I knew not to yell for Tess. She was often not there. Our Tess needed to roam. But I heard Betty calling for her.

"Get up! Fire! *Ruuuuun!*"

We stumbled in the blackness, bumping into furniture, kicking and shoving things out of our way. I was kicked and shoved. It didn't matter. Words ran into and past each other. Voices were indistinguishable in the smoke and fear.

"What's happening?"

"Oh my god! What? Is that smoke?"

"So much smoke! Ow!"

"Is Tess back?"

"You're on my nightgown. Let go!"

"Move it! Get out of my way."

"Where is it?"

"What about my stuff?"

"Are we all here?"

"I *said* let go!"

And then, over and over, "Who's got the Little Ones?"

"It's okay—Joe's rounding them up," Betty and I took turns repeating. "We've to get down to the main floor and wait."

Then we heard Joe's hoarse, singsongy Southern voice floating up through the stairwell. "Hold hands, little ladies, hold hands. Two by two, two by two. Just like we practiced. There you go. Don't ya worry. You'll see the Seven in the main hall."

The Little Ones didn't scream or cry out. Were they less afraid than I was?

"Quick now, ladies!" He clapped his hands. "That's right, good girls."

We clambered down the steps ahead of the Little Ones. Down one floor, then another. They traipsed down behind us. When we got to the back hall, Tess had appeared like a smoke spirit. How?

We stood against the walls. Just like in the drills. Joe lead a procession of little nightgowns. "Mary, you just hold on tight to Mr. Joe's hand," he said.

Mary was a little slow in so many little ways. But she was everyone's favorite. We waited for them to pass while the smoke stung our eyes. They wanted a hug from us, a comforting squeeze, a pat, but knew they dared not risk it. They stayed in their two-by-two formations.

"What's that smell?"

"I feel sick."

"Why is it smoky?"

"Why are the Seven just standing there?"

"I can't breathe."

"My doll!"

"I want to hold Julie's hand."

"You're squeezing too hard."

"My nose smells bad."

Not one asked for her mother. Why would they? This and the weight of the darkness pressed me into the wall.

"They're out!"

Now it was our turn. We began our exit, some hand in hand, some arm in arm, some alone. The floor was warm on our still-bare feet. Fear rose off of us in plumes, blending into the smoke that had followed us down the stairs. Too slow. Somebody shouted, "Move it!"

It may have been me.

We were chased by the fire, but we didn't run. We walked smartly down the hall. Like we'd been taught to do. When we had to be, when it counted, we were good.

We walked past the receiving room and the common room, which was for home and visual arts. I glanced in and made out the ghost outlines of the Singer sewing machine, two easels, the stools, all seven of them. They were waiting for us to sit and tease each other, to laugh and pout, to misbehave, at which time Miss Webster would summon Mrs. Hazelton. She was always called as a last resort. Mrs. Hazelton would pretend to be cross, and we would pretend to behave for the rest of the day.

I knew enough to whisper, "Goodbye."

Through the large double front doors and onto the verandah we trooped, silent now. The floorboards were cool here and damp on our feet. All of us stopped as one, blinking at the moonlight. We had to will our eyes to see. Mrs. Hazelton had joined Joe and Miss Webster on the front lawn, far away from the burning building, almost at the circular drive. The grass bathed our feet in dew as we went to them.

The Little Ones finally started crying. Not all, but most. Now fully awake, they were shivering and afraid. And I felt as if I was still dreaming, even though I knew I wasn't. I was protected this way. In my dreams I got out, survived. In my fire dreams, I was smarter and stronger, braver than I really was. When I was awake, I pretended.

"It'll be okay," I said to Betty. "It will be okay." I turned to the others, smiling and pretending again. I caught Sara's attention. Her eyes were wide, full of the night and panic, but she nodded, tried to smile. "I heard Joe say that the firemen are on their way," she said.

This moved like a snake among all the orphans.

"Jumpin' Joe called the firemen."

"The firemen are coming."

"All the firemen from town are coming. All the volunteers too."

"Here come the firemen!"

"I hear the trucks. Can you hear the trucks?"

But the trucks did not come. Not then.

The fire came.

The flames burst through the third floor in the very back of the building, tossing roof tiles out of its way. Sparks broke free, heading upward like inverted shooting stars. We could hear the screeching of the pipes as they distorted into new shapes, the roar and sigh of the timbers just before they fell. And then the flames reached for heaven but only managed to lick the very bottom of a black velvet sky.

"Ooooooh!" gasped the Little Ones. Joe made a sign of the cross. I never took him for a Papist. And here I thought I knew him.

The noises were terrifying. A fire is a loud thing. Aside from the wail of the pipes, we heard it chomp on plaster and furniture and electrical wires. It shoved things out of its way so that it could breathe better. Wood crackled, then snapped, then crashed, and the Little Ones clung to us. And still it got bigger, got greedier.

"It's in our room," whispered Betty.

I reached for her. "They'll be here soon. It will be *fine*. We will all be fine."

"Then why are you crying?" she asked.

I think I knew it was coming. That it was going to happen before it happened. First came the moan, the orphanage surrendering, then the explosion, in time with the one in my heart. *No.* Not again. I was there on the wet grass and I was in the dream, the bad one. The windows blew out in the third floor. Our room, our windows. Like before.

And the glass shattered.

"No!" I pushed the Little Ones away.

There was more screaming. The trucks were coming. The bells were ringing. The glass was shattering.

My heart broke out of my chest.

The glass was shattering.

"Toni, stop!"

"Toni, come back!"

"Toni!" Matron, Joe, the Little Ones and Betty were all calling. The Seven yelled; some came after me. "Toni, stop, will you!"

"Toni!"

But the glass was shattering.

And I had to run. I ran to the river. I ran faster and faster, but not so fast that I didn't hear the singing.

Ridiculous.

Our home was burning and the orphans were singing "Amazing Grace," of all the stupid, stupid things. But still, I slowed down just enough to catch up to the words, and then I sang right along with them.

"Have I the Right?"

(THE HONEYCOMBS)

AS THE DAWN broke, panic crashed against me like waves smashing against a boulder. Then again, I'd never seen the ocean, so what did I know? Still, I bet that's what it felt like. I stared at the sputtering river, trying to calm the pounding within me. It wasn't a dream.

It happened.

It's okay. We're all okay. I said it over and over, like a prayer. I'd been praying for hours. This was my safe place, sitting on the riverbank, under the willow in the woods near the orphanage. They all knew I did this. Well, the Seven knew, and so did Joe.

Get up, Toni. Time to go back. Time to see…what?

The voice inside called it like it was. *Coward.* Shame nipped at my heels as I made my way to Mrs. Hazelton's cottage. Her place was far enough away from the orphanage that I figured it would be okay. That she would be okay. That she would know what to do now.

Please.

The rest of the Seven and the Little Ones would be at the church. That was the drill: *Should an emergency occur at the orphanage, you are all to make your way over to St. Jerome's Anglican church in Hope. The good reverend will know what to do.*

I wondered whether the good reverend knew what to do now.

"Toni, praise the Lord!"

Miss Webster scooped me up and into her substantial self. This was startling. Miss Webster was by no means an affectionate woman. She hustled me onto the verandah, clucking, cooing and chiding the whole way. "You gave us such a fright, dear. Mrs. Hazelton, here she is! Our Toni's here! Mrs. Hazelton!"

Mrs. Hazelton, our matron, stepped out her front door, which had been left wide open. She looked like she didn't know whether to hit me or hug me. Against her better judgment, she reached out and embraced me. It had been such a long time since I had been held, not since I was one of the Little Ones. She was as frail as tissue paper in my arms. That scared me.

"I'm sorry, ma'am. I'm so, so sorry."

"Toni, my dear! Joe said not to worry, but...but...how could you! How...never mind, you're wet with the damp. I've laid out a uniform for you from one of our former charges—shoes, socks, everything—hanging in the bathroom, that first door down the hall." She let go of me, but then grabbed both of my hands. "It's been quite a night. Change, Toni, and then come into my study. I'll have some tea and toast waiting."

"Yes, ma'am." I couldn't stop shivering. "Thank you, ma'am. The others?"

"They are all at the church where they *should* be. They will be coming over later—at least, the Seven will. We have much to discuss." She sighed. "In a way, I'm glad that you're the first."

The first?

She pushed me toward the bathroom, which had been one of the great mysteries of our world if only because none of us had ever been in there. Over the years we'd all had cause to be in Mrs. Hazleton's study for various "talks." Some of us more than others. I was there a fair bit. It usually had to do with my attitude and/or deportment. Many things would be expressed in a firm tone, accompanied by a fair bit of sighing and eyebrow raising. This would be followed by excessive promising and apologizing on my part. Attitude or not, not even I had ever dared to use her bathroom. It was one of the unwritten rules: no one goes, even if you have to go.

I gasped when I opened the door. The inner sanctum was everything we'd ever imagined it would be. There was a dainty claw-foot bathtub and a really fancy pedestal sink. A purple bar of soap sat in a curlicued china soap dish. Lavender? The aroma made me dizzy. The whole room was covered in red and pink cabbage-rose wallpaper, with curtains that matched exactly. Pink, puffy towels were draped precisely over elaborate brass towel holders. I didn't know that towels could look like that. *Do I dare? No, absolutely not.* I let my face and hands air-dry after I washed up. I just stood there, swallowed up by all those roses, and fretted about dripping on the fluffy bath mat. The shirt, uniform jumper and underthings were all much too large, as were the shoes, and I was one of the taller girls. Whoever used to wear this must have been one substantial girl. I combed my memory. Peggy! She'd left years and years ago, but the Seven had always got her confused with the staff, she was that hefty. Where had Peggy gone?

Where would I go?

I rebraided my hair, smoothed my eyebrows with a lick on my finger and, when I could no longer postpone the inevitable, made my way to the study.

Mrs. Hazelton, as always, was behind her beautiful polished desk. She was dwarfed by the large leather chair that I swear she used to fill up. When did she shrink? Her desk, usually immaculate, was smothered with papers, ledgers, binders, boxes and envelopes. "Sit down, Toni, and please help yourself to the toast and tea on the side table."

I poured the tea and smeared the toast with butter and huge dollops of jam. Rather than drawing a reprimand, my greediness made her smile. "Go on, Toni, put in all the sugar and milk you want. I know you like it sweet." I helped myself to three extra spoonfuls, hardly feeling guilty at all.

She watched me gulp down two cups of tea and four pieces of toast. She also watched as a large drop of raspberry jam rolled off the toast and landed on Peggy's immaculately clean uniform. She saw it but pretended not to.

"Feeling better?" she said after I'd eaten the last crumbs.

"Yes, ma'am. You said something about me being the first?"

She nodded and turned to the window. "Yes, yes I did. Well, it's no secret that the Home has been winding down for the past several years. You all know that we haven't been accepting new charges in quite some time. In fact, the times have been changing all around us." She made a face. "Hideous bureaucratic nightmares are replacing homes such as ours."

She was in preamble mode. I *hated* preamble. Especially when I didn't understand it. I wanted everyone to get to the point instantly or sooner. This was where I would usually have interrupted and gotten myself in trouble. Instead, I stared at the bright-red jam dot decorating my lap and realized to my horror that I really had to use the bathroom. I was afraid to before, and now, with all the tea...

"So, even given this horrendous event, I—we—have had quite some time to prepare for this, Antoinette."

Uh-oh. I was only "Antoinette" when I was in serious trouble.

"Actually"—she turned to me again—"I have been preparing for you Seven almost from the beginning. You are my very special senior girls."

"Yes, ma'am, that's very kind of you, and don't think for a minute that we don't appreciate it."

She shook her head. "You have, at times, a certain charm about you, Toni. It will serve you well." She leaned into her desk. Papers fluttered to the floor in protest. She didn't seem to notice. This was all wrong.

"I have to attend to my health, you see. So I won't be directing the changeover. Our board of directors will appoint a trustee to oversee the process. The Little Ones will be placed in foster care." Again, she made a face. "Homes will be found for each of them."

"Homes? You mean adoption?" My heart soared.

"Well no, not exactly, maybe, eventually…" She paused and looked at the mess of papers on her desk as if she was surprised to see it. "But not for the Seven, Toni. You see, you are all of an age…even Malou is sixteen now. You're almost seventeen, Sara is eighteen, Betty is seventeen, and…"

"With respect, ma'am, I know how old we are!" I jumped up. "What about us? What's going to happen to us?"

"Ah, there's my Toni."

She meant the reckless Toni.

"You will be just fine. Sit down, Antoinette." She sat back and seemed to study me. "How much do you want to know about who you really are?"

"Ma'am?" I fell back into my chair. I knew who I was.

"It's not much, but it's the best I can offer, my dear. That and some money." She rubbed her forehead. "It is the least I can do."

"Ma'am?" She wasn't making any sense.

"There are no provisions for the Seven aside from what I have been able to save for you over the years. You are of age." She sighed and paused. "I have set aside a sum of money to help each of you on your way. If you're careful, it should take you to your destination and aid with food and lodging for quite some time."

"My destination? Excuse me, but…"

"What I am about to give you, Toni, is highly irregular and quite possibly illegal." Mrs. Hazelton raised her hand as if to ward off more words. "You see, I have items from when each of you came into the orphanage. They may hold clues to your identity, perhaps to whatever family you have left out there."

"My family! My mother? You mean the woman who almost killed me *before* she abandoned me?" I embraced myself as if to shield the scars that were still there underneath Peggy's extra-large uniform. "The crazy lady who cut and—"

"Calm down, Antoinette. You don't know that. We don't anything for sure. Allow me to finish."

My head pounded. "Yes, ma'am." *What* was happening?

"You're a strong and capable worker. Your skills in the kitchen and in serving will stand you in good stead. You have a lot to thank Joseph for."

Was I supposed to sling hash alongside Sara at Loretta's Diner, Hope's sole dining establishment?

"These skills will be useful to you in Toronto. I have no doubts that you will thrive. I have a bus schedule here."

"Toronto! Wait. What? Toronto?" I stood up again.

"Sit down, Toni. Yes, Toronto. It's on the hospital-release form. Sit."

I stayed standing. Mrs. Hazelton shook her head as she reached into a drawer and pulled out a beat-up, old manila envelope. She handed it to me.

"Yes, Toronto." She raised her hand to her forehead. "I'm sorry, dear, but there's very little for you here in Hope—for all of the Seven. I did my best, but as it stands... You can all stay a few days at the church, but..." Again she paused, seeming to search for words. Mrs. Hazelton never had to search for words. "I believe that the few items I have for you lead you directly to Toronto, and even to a certain area within the city. I've looked into it. There are three buses that leave each day from town, or you can, as you know, flag the bus down on the road. The bus leaves at 9:40 AM, 12:40 PM and 4:40 PM. The money is in a smaller envelope inside, and then there's your..." She stopped to cough. "Well, all that I have for you—your identifying clues. Clues to who you are, Toni. You need to sit, dear."

I sat at the edge of my seat, trying to locate my breath. I couldn't, so I focused on her instead. She didn't look good, and I didn't feel good. I fumbled with the manila envelope; my fingers felt like bricks. Aside from the money envelope, three things fell into my lap. Three pieces of me. Mrs. Hazelton leaned back in her chair and waited.

There was a much-folded, small white sheet, now sticky with raspberry jam.

Release Form: Antoinette Royce
Birth Date: September 13, 1947
Released From Toronto General Hospital: April 30, 1950
Admission: Smoke inhalation, extensive lacerations, spleen removal
Follow-up: Released to Dr. Reginald G. Blunt, The Benevolent Home for Necessitous Girls, Hope, Ontario.
Mother: Halina Royce
Father: Unknown

Royce? My surname was Royce? Really? Royce? We girls had each been given surnames when we arrived at the orphanage. Mrs. Hazelton had christened the Seven with ones she had pulled from *Anne of Green Gables*. Until that very moment I had been Antoinette Cuthbert.

And that was only the beginning. There were so many shocks from so few words.

Extensive lacerations, smoke inhalation? Was there a fire?

Spleen removal? Wait, whoa, hang on—they took out my spleen? What *was* a spleen?

Wait, wait. *Mother: Halina Royce.*

Mother.

The word made me woozy and angry at the same time. "My *mother*, was she, is she...?"

"I don't know, dear. No one does. Did she survive her injuries, if she had any? Did she just…perhaps it was all too much for her, whatever it was. We don't know. Toni, I would tell you if I knew. All we know is that you were transported here before your fourth birthday."

It was too much. No more, no more. The room spun.

"Excuse me, I have to use your, um, go to the…I'll be right back."

I ran to the bathroom and used the toilet this time. I splashed water on my face, washed my hands with her purple soap and dried myself with the fat fluffy towel. I wanted to stay in there forever. Outside, out there, was impossible. I repeated the whole process two more times before I found the courage to drag myself back.

Mrs. Hazelton had not moved, yet she looked even smaller than she had a few minutes ago. The next item I picked up was a torn menu from some restaurant called the Noronic. It was yellowed and stained, but the featured menu of the day was still clearly visible. The appetizers were *Oysters Rockefeller*, the main was *Dover Sole Almandine with Potatoes Gratin*, and the dessert was *Baked Alaska*. Despite all my years in the kitchen with Joe and all that he had taught me, I didn't know what a single one of those things was.

What kind of pathetic clue was an old menu?

The last piece was an ancient playbill like the little posters you'd see around town for Harvest Festival, only this one featured a jazz band, the Smokers, in a club called Willa's on Gerrard Street in Toronto.

And that was it. The sum total of me and all that I was, on three useless pieces of paper. Words were spoken by Mrs. Hazelton, many more words, but I heard only some of them. I was to receive a small suitcase, which would be filled with "items of necessity" donated by the nice church ladies. They had been working through the night. I knew from her tone that I was supposed to be filled with gratitude.

Gratitude eluded me. It eluded me even when she went to her shelves and extracted a book, *Immortal Poems of the English Language*. "Miss Webster said that you were always sneaking off with the library copy. This one is mine, Toni. Now it's yours." She placed it on my lap. It felt like a brick.

I didn't thank her. I didn't have any words. I will burn in hell.

"I know this is a shock, dear. Each of the Seven will have similar meetings with me. Each of you will have a journey ahead. That is, if you so choose."

Choose? What choice? I may have said that part out loud.

Every so often, I stood and was told to sit again.

"Be very, very careful with the money. You mustn't let anyone see it."

I stood up.

"Sit down. Don't talk to anybody at the bus station, especially men. This is important. I cannot stress that enough. Toronto is a big city and sometimes a dangerous one for pretty young girls. Certain types of men sometimes patrol the bus depot—bad men. You understand, dear?"

I didn't have a clue what she was talking about, but I nodded.

"You will be fine, Toni. You, my dear, are made for the world, a bigger world."

Did I nod again?

Finally, it was over. I knew because I stood up and Mrs. Hazelton didn't tell me to sit right down again. I walked over to her. She hugged me, and it felt like she would splinter in my embrace. But I didn't want to let go.

There isn't an orphan alive who isn't hurting for a hug.

"Don't Let the Sun Catch You Crying"

(GERRY AND THE PACEMAKERS)

HOW CAN YOUR life be one way one minute and then completely different the next? It's not possible.

Is it?

Betty was right outside the door. I grabbed her and held on. "I don't know what to say."

"It's going to be all right." She hugged me tighter.

"No, you don't understand. It's..."

Mrs. Hazelton opened the door. "Betty, please come in."

"We'll talk before I go," I promised and kissed her cheek. What a liar I was.

I was greeted by squeals from Tess and Cady, who were milling around the living room under Miss Webster's watchful eye. They scolded me and hugged me and then scolded me some more. A thousand questions. What could I say? Where to begin?

Miss Webster stepped over and pulled me aside. "Your suitcase is ready on the verandah. You can spend the night at the church and leave tomorrow or the next day or the day after that. You can leave whenever you want. I'm sure you want to talk it all over with the girls, say a proper goodbye."

Did I?

Dot joined us in the living room. She smiled, but then looked unsure what to make of Miss Webster hovering over me and moved to the others. Malou and Sara would arrive soon, I was sure. *We are the Seven.*

We *were* the Seven.

Everybody would leave, blown apart by the fire. I turned to watch them huddling on Mrs. Hazelton's sofa, trying to make sense of it. They didn't know anything yet.

The weight of them, of their goodbyes, would crush me. I couldn't do it.

The first bus to Toronto would be leaving from Hope within the hour. I could flag it down in front of the orphanage—what was left of the orphanage. I stood swaying beside Miss Webster for what seemed like hours, trying to decide. Tess beckoned me to come and sit. We could write to each other. Mrs. Hazelton had said that we could use Loretta's Diner as a postal drop; the letters would be forwarded as soon as we had addresses. I could do that, yes, and I'd explain that it was too hard to say goodbye... that I had to run. Again.

Tess patted a corner of the sofa. She knew I liked to sit on the end. There were a million things that they knew about me, accepted about me, and that from now on, no one would know.

I couldn't do it. I pulled Miss Webster toward the door.

"I'll be leaving on the 9:40 bus this morning, Miss Webster." She shook her head but kept silent. "I don't think I can...please let them know. Tell Betty I'll write." I wanted to tell her to tell each of them that I loved them. But the words got stuck in my throat.

"Toni? Are you sure? Don't be impulsive. Goodbyes are certainly painful, but I'm sure that..." Then she caught herself. "No, I understand. Truly, I do. I will tell them; don't you worry." She smiled when she saw the poetry book. "At least you'll have your very own copy. Go, Toni, go with God, and safe travels."

"Yes, ma'am. Thank you, ma'am. I didn't even... Mrs. Hazelton...please thank her."

I ducked out to the verandah before tears had a chance to form. A small suitcase more like a carpetbag, a thing from another century, waited for me by the nearest chair. I shoved my book and the envelope on top without even glancing at the contents of the bag.

I picked it up and walked into a yawning sky. My feet slid forward and back into Peggy's too-large shoes. I tried to grip them with my toes, but that made walking even more awkward, so I settled into a step, slide, step, slide. The cloying, singed odor of a drowned fire choked me within a minute of leaving the cottage. I marched on, trying to breathe through my mouth. When I got closer to the orphanage, I heard the shouts of the firemen, but I didn't turn to look. I refused to acknowledge the charred carcass of my home, our home. I continued my ungainly march far to the right of the orphanage with my eyes trained straight ahead. I marched past the building, past the firemen and the officials, past our beautiful front lawn and the large circular drive where most of us had learned to ride a bike, the senior girls always teaching the Little Ones in an unbroken pattern. I marched straight to the road. Brave, fierce and alone.

Except that I wasn't any of those things. A figure as slight as a pen stroke waited on the side of the roadway. I knew that lanky body of bones was deceiving. I'd seen it heave fifty-pound sacks of potatoes like they were filled with cotton puffs. Jumpin' Joe stood silhouetted by the morning sun, arms crossed. He was still, for once. Of all the people I could not bear to say goodbye to, Joe and Betty were the hardest.

I knew he was smiling even as I stared at my feet.

"Shoes too big for you, girl?"

"Yes, sir." Now I was addressing *his* shoes. Shame is a heavy thing. It wouldn't allow me to raise my head.

"Shoot, girl. Since when have you been *sirring* me?" He shook his head. "Thought you'd get by me, eh?"

"Yes, sir." The back of my eyes burned.

"Hey, child, remember the song? What did it teach us? The sun's shining, ain't it?"

"Don't let the sun catch you crying," I answered as I threw myself at him. "I'm sorry, Joe. I couldn't, just couldn't, not them and not you, especially not you. I couldn't say goodbye. I can't...I'm—I'm so sorry."

"Don't you think I knew that? I ain't judging, little spit-fire. I'm here to give ya something." He fumbled with his jacket pocket. "I got to this and a couple other things before the firemen hosed the crap out of my room."

Joe held out the small aquamarine transistor radio on which we had religiously listened to Top 40 hits for all the years I had worked in the kitchen. Each morning at dawn, Joe would come into the kitchen with his radio, and each evening, after we had cleaned up and prepped for the next day, Joe took it back to his room. At night he could catch some of the American signals and reach his beloved jazz stations in Buffalo.

"Take it, girl."

I shook my head. "No, Joe, I can't." The little radio was everything to him. "I won't."

He spat on the ground. Joe spat a lot. It gave Miss Webster the vapors. "Shoot, I ain't giving you my guitar. It's just a radio. Hold it for me then. I'll be coming your way eventually. Gonna get back into my own music scene. I'll be doing that when things here get locked up." He spat again. He was aiming for an upturned turtle shell two yards away and nailed it. Joe said that everyone from Louisiana could spit-nail *anything, anywheres, anytime*. "So you'd be doing me a favor, see? Stick it in that fancy carpetbagger valise ya got there."

I obeyed silently.

"And don't talk to any menfolk, especially in the—"

"Bus depot," I finished for him. "Yeah, Mrs. Hazelton went on and on—"

"Hey, girl!" He took my arm. "This is serious like. Keep your eyes open out there. Promise!"

"Sure, Joe, you know me—I'm real smart." Or I would be when I got to where I was going. Yeah, that was right. I *would* be. Hey, anything was possible from here on in. I could be a new me, the real me! Well, as soon as I figured out who the real me was I could.

He looked worried. "Yeah, you're smart but not as smart as ya think ya are. You kids, ya just don't know what ya don't know, and it pains me."

"I'll be fine. Mrs. Hazelton said so!"

He spat again. "'Course ya will."

We spied the bus, a gray dot breaking through a wavy horizon. Joe tried to press a folded five-dollar bill into my hand. "It's for the fare and getting you to where ya gots to go once ya get there."

"No, Joe, I've got money! I'm sure it's lots. It's in an envelope that—"

"Yeah, child, I know all about your big envelope, and I know about the money. You got yourself $138. Guard it with your life, little girl. The bus fare ought not to be no more than $2.75. Don't let 'em cheat ya, hear?"

"Joe, you need—"

"Antoinette! I ain't never hit a woman in all my born days, but I'm willing to make an exception, right here, right now."

We smiled at each other. There wasn't a day that went by that Joe wouldn't threaten me with that exact same line, several times an hour.

"Yes, boss."

He flagged down the Greyhound.

The bus rolled to a stop, kicking up dust and gravel. The door opened with a mighty wheeze. "Joe, I'm…" I threw myself at him. I was going to disintegrate.

"Shhh. Remember, the sun's shining, girl. No tears."

"Yes, sir. Thank you, Joe. I promise." I turned my back on him as soon as I kissed his grizzled cheek.

I paid my fare, collected the change and made my way to the nearest empty seat. I did not look out the window. I did not look back. I stared at the back of the seat right in front of me. And still it didn't matter. The new me was going to be smart and fearless and sassy, but the old me didn't stop crying until we got to Toronto.

"Walk On By"

(DIONNE WARWICK)

AN ELDERLY GENTLEMAN in a seat down and across the aisle from me offered up a clean white handkerchief. "Keep it," he said before returning to his seat. I didn't even say thank you. I seemed to be incapable of thanking anybody for anything. Mrs. Hazelton would have been mortified. I was mortified. Twenty minutes away from the orphanage and my manners were already shredded.

Even I knew my reaction to leaving didn't make any kind of sense. I had plotted and dreamed about getting away from the orphanage and all its rules and isolation for forever. Most of the others dreamed about finding their *true* mothers, who would, of course, be impossibly glamorous women who had somehow misplaced their offspring. The Seven would trace and weave convoluted stories to explain away the sins of their parents. I'd weave with them some of the time, even though I knew my mother was a monster and the last person in the world I'd want to find if she was still breathing.

In my dreams, she had hurt me badly. Dreams or memory? Either way, I was not interested in finding her.

So I'd fake it, pretend to get all moony and emotional along with the others. *Ya goes along to get along*, as Joe would say. But I'd never do it again. I wouldn't have to. I didn't care about the story of my parents. Did I? No. They hurt me. They left me. Period.

Three lousy pieces of paper. It figured.

When we were really little, Betty would get going with her favorite fantasies. She'd build elaborate stories about how we'd for sure get adopted by the same loving family and grow up as sisters with everyone admiring us. I knew better. My body was heavily scarred. No decent family would want me. I didn't want me. Most of the marks were barely visible now. Only the faintest ice-pink ridges stained my shoulders, neck, arms and part of my torso. When my mind was clean and free of fear, I saw that. When it wasn't, I was that little girl again, the one covered in scars inflicted by her mother.

My fantasy had been to leave, to get away from the orphanage. But on that bus, as I blubbered into that man's hanky, I would have sold my soul to be right back there at the orphanage, back with Mrs. Hazelton, with the Seven and with Joe.

A man never knows what he wants until he loses it. It was another one of Joe's sayings. Joe had a million of them. Most of them were eyeball rollers, but every so often he nailed it like spit.

With a shock, I realized that the bus must have stopped. People were getting up and fetching their things from the overhead bins. I stopped sniffling and quickly opened up a small note that Joe had folded into his five-dollar bill. I hadn't been able to bring myself to read it earlier. I didn't even know that Joe could write. As it turned out, he could and he couldn't.

You go strait to the Dundas subway stayshun. I have talked to you about the subways many times. Pay your fair and go till the Bloor stop. You can walk to Yorkville from their. Ask some nice lady how. Theirs lots of rooms to rent and lots of cafes their to. Get a job in one. Write as soon as your settled.

Yes, Joe, okay, I thought. I'll be okay. I clutched the piece of paper. There wasn't a moment to linger. Everyone was already up and off the bus. I grabbed my bag and stepped into pandemonium.

The entire city of Toronto must have been in that terminal. There was row upon slanted row of Greyhound buses, like a herd of behemoths both disgorging and swallowing people at an alarming rate. The newly ejected headed to a large hall, and I fell into their swirling mass. It was worse inside. Aside from the snaking lines of people who were waiting to purchase tickets, there were people shouting and screaming all around me. Some were crying because they were leaving, but most seemed to be crying because they had been reunited with their people.

They had folks waiting on them.

Millions of people were crowded into that vast cavern of a place, yet I'd never felt so alone in my life. Joe would have said, "Get your girdle on, girl!" That meant to stand up straight and face what you had to face. I tried. I failed. I mean, how was I supposed to even find the *Dundas subway*?

A man came up to me. "Hey, little chickie, lost your way?" He was pleasant-looking and very finely groomed, but he *was* a man.

I froze.

All the adults had warned me off speaking to strange men. But then again, since when did I pay 100 percent attention to what the adults told me to do?

He walked all the way around me. "You look Irish, black Irish. There's a call for that, pretty girl like you. Fresh out of the convent, are you?"

Convent? Did I look like a nun in Peggy's billowing uniform? I felt heat rising to my face, but I held my tongue.

"Looks like you could be a dancer under all of that. Would you like that? Ever heard of Zanzibar's, Irish? It's famous—ask anyone. I'm like an agent. Can you dance?"

Could I dance? How could he tell? I loved to dance! Should I show him? When I danced, I forgot who I was or wasn't. I'd danced to Top 40 tunes while peeling potatoes, scrubbing pots and stirring oatmeal. Joe would show me moves. *Nobody* moved like Joe. He'd show me and then I'd show the Seven later when we were supposed to be asleep.

I could be a dancer? Wait, did he say I was pretty?

Stop. He was a man *and* he was talking *and* this was a bus depot. Everyone had been very clear on that point. But to be a dancer...

"Maybe you're one of them Mennonites, Irish. If you can't dance, they'll teach you. The main thing is, you got the look, if you know what I mean."

What look? Sweat gathered under the braid on my neck and then began to dribble down into Peggy's underthings.

"Cat got your tongue, Irish?" He reached for my arm.

"Leave her be, jerk, or I'll call the cops." It was a girl—no, a woman, but a young one. She stepped right on over to him bold as brass. Even more shocking was the way she was dressed. I'd never seen anyone who looked like that. Her skirt was shorter than the shirt I wore under Peggy's uniform! There were no pleats on it; it was just a piece of fabric stretched across her thighs. Her knees were showing! The skirt, such as it was, had bold, thick stripes in colors that God never intended to go together. She wore this floaty orange blouse, and she was all done up like the photographs pasted on the storefront at Stella's Beauty Emporium back home. "Beat it!" she snarled.

Well, the man didn't beat anything, but he did disappear into the crowd.

As soon as she'd chased him off, she turned to me. "What a creep! You okay?"

Instead of answering or thanking her, I blurted out, "Gosh, you're beautiful!" And *gosh*, I sounded like an idiot.

"I'll tell my boyfriend you said so when I see him in Simcoe." At least she didn't laugh at me. "Do you know where you're going? Kids like you come through here all the time and…it's best if you've got somewhere to go."

"Oh yes." I showed her Joe's note and then became embarrassed for both him and me at the same time. "His spelling's a bit off."

She glanced at her watch. "Okay. Come on, I'll point you in the right direction. I don't want you to get confused down there. The Dundas station is yellow and so is Bloor. There are other colors in between. He's right about getting a place in Yorkville; it's going to be a happening place." We walked a block or two and then she pointed me to stairs that led underground. "You'll see a map and a place to pay your fare. Have a gas!" she said before melting back into the crowd.

"Thank you!"

I barely survived the whoosh of the subway trip. It felt like a rocket ship. Nobody else seemed to be worried, so I tried hard to button myself down. I examined my fellow astronauts. I saw another girl dressed sort of like my bus-depot savior, and another older lady who was actually wearing purple pants with a jacket to match. Other ladies wore very fitted dresses that flared out at the hips in a dizzying array of patterns and colors. The men, too, those not in suits, wore pullovers and shirts in every shade under the sun. Well, if nothing else, Toronto sure was a colorful place. This would be fine. I would be fine. Better than fine.

Except my hands trembled so much that I gripped my bag tighter still.

Surely anyone would find the subway a terrifying experience. I mean, it was underground, for heaven's sake! What if you had to get off? What if you missed your stop? What if it halted in one of the never-ending tunnels? What if there was a stampede to get off? I swear, there were more people in this one subway car than there were in the entire town of Hope.

This would be fine. I would be fine. Better than fine.

Between the sheer speed of the subway and my taking in the things people wore and repeating my mantra, I did almost miss my stop. I emerged on Bloor, blinded by sunlight. I had to ask a number of ladies to direct me to Yorkville. They were mostly helpful, but I'd get myself turned around by the blocks and the sheer number of people around me within minutes of each set of directions.

When I finally found Yorkville Avenue, it was almost four o'clock. Tea and toast with Mrs. Hazelton seemed like a lifetime ago. I knocked on every door that had a Room to Let sign. There were lots and lots of signs, but I was turned away again and again. *I don't truck in runaways*, they'd say as they shut the door in my face before I had a chance to explain. Even though the houses were a bit shabby and run-down in a squished-together-tight kind of way, the actual street was a party. All sorts of people milled around or sat in groups on the stoops, laughing. Still, when the sixth door slammed in my face, it shook me to the core.

Fear crawled in with the hunger, and they both grumbled ominously in my stomach.

I'll be fine… The seventh door slammed. What would Joe tell me to do? *Use that thick smart head of yours, girl.* The eighth door didn't even open, but I saw a lady peeking out of her lace curtains. She shooed me away with her hand.

I finally wised up by the ninth place. It was on Hazelton Avenue, as if Mrs. Hazelton had a whole street named after her. It had to be a good omen. I inhaled as I knocked on number 75. The freshly painted cherry-red door cracked open just as far as the chain lock would allow.

"Yeah?"

"Good afternoon, ma'am. I'm not a runaway and I have money. I'm here about the room."

The door opened—I mean, all the way—and holy smoke, it was like Marilyn Monroe was on the other side. The woman wore a very tight black dress that scooped down rather shamelessly in the front. A cigarette hung from the reddest lips I'd ever seen. Bar none, she was the most glamorous woman in the world. What a city!

"You got some ID, kid?"

"I don't know, ma'am. Maybe. It's possible. What is that?"

"*Identification.*" She started to close the door.

To have come so close…"Wait. Please!" I opened my little carpetbag and riffled through the manila envelope until I found the release form, still proudly sporting the raspberry-jam stain. I handed it to her.

"Geez, kid, you're an orphan?"

"Yes, ma'am. But the orphanage burned down. I'm here to find a job, maybe in a café, and, well, maybe my family too."

Was I? Wow, I was. Yeah, I *was*. I came to know it by saying it. If I was going to find the *real* me, I'd have to find out where the real me came from, right? I don't know, it just felt like the right thing to say.

"The orphanage burned down? Holy Hannah, you sure you're not starring in a movie?"

"Ma'am?"

She sighed and shook her head. "Okay, okay. I know I'm going to regret this, but come on in, Orphan Annie. I want two weeks rent up front. I get paid every week on the Sunday and not a day later, hear?"

"Toni."

"Huh?"

"It's Orphan Toni, ma'am. Antoinette Royce." Royce. It was the first time I had used my newfound surname. It felt like I was wearing somebody else's clothes, which, when you think about it, I was.

"Ha!" She slapped me on the back. "Well, welcome to Toronto, Orphan Toni."

I shuffled into a narrow hallway with a very ornate but equally narrow staircase. A gigantic crystal ashtray decorated the top of a covered radiator. "Your room is at the top of the stairs. It's the biggest and the prettiest room, but don't get all excited—it's also the hottest in the summer and coldest in the winter." My new landlady stubbed out one lipstick-stained cigarette and quickly lit another, with an intricate gold lighter. "It's five dollars a week, fully furnished. Bathroom's on the second floor, and you only have to share it with the professor. He's my only other tenant."

I think that was supposed to be my cue to exclaim how wonderful it sounded. But I was too hungry, too relieved and too bone weary to do so. When I didn't say anything, she narrowed her eyes. "You do your own tidying and linen laundry though. I don't look like a cleaning lady, do I?"

"No, ma'am, you look like a movie star."

My landlady patted white-blond hair that did not budge in the patting. "Everybody says that." But she appeared to be pleased with me again. "My name's Grady." She removed a key from a key ring that was hanging on the wall. "Go on, check it out. I'll be up to collect the rent in a minute, and I'll show you the ropes."

Three long flights later, I turned the key in the door to my room.

Wow. It was huge. The ceiling slanted down in places, but the room was full of light and the wallpaper had a cheerful paisley pattern. It was almost as perfect as Mrs. Hazelton's bathroom. No, it was more perfect. It was mine. There was a cast-iron bed covered in a patchwork quilt, a nightstand with a lamp, and a bureau with an actual mirror on it. In the corner farthest away from the window there was a little sink with a bit of a counter right beside it.

A hot plate stood on it, with a small pot beckoning to me. I couldn't remember ever being hungrier. The rafters and wallpaper swirled as I dropped my bag. I'd lived a lifetime in the past twenty-four hours. The fire, the river, Mrs. Hazelton's envelope, sneaking away from the Seven, the bus ride, the strange man at the depot, the subway and finally this. I had made it. I lay down, in Peggy's clothes and all. I didn't even know—or care—what else was in the bag. I just lay down. There was time.

I had made it.

"Needles and Pins"

(THE SEARCHERS)

MY LANDLADY'S FULL name was Mrs. Grady Eleanor Vespucci. "The Eleanor is silent—remember that. The rest is Italian and Irish, or, in other words, wop and mick stuck together, and a deadlier combo was never born and should never have married, I might add. Sit, sit." She waved at a beautifully carved chesterfield. "When I came upstairs last evening, you were passed out cold. So I thought, what the hell, eh, and here we are now."

Mrs. Vespucci was "entertaining" me in her front parlor. She kept reminding me that this wasn't going to be a regular occurrence. "Don't get used to it, kid." Tea and toast. Again. Even though my head was spinning with the newness of it all, I remembered to come down with my rent money and to stay away from the jam.

"I don't mean to pry," she said, eyeing my now-wrinkled uniform, "but is that all you got to wear?" It was like Peggy's uniform was a personal affront of some kind. "Look, the

coffeehouses aren't bars—they don't have liquor licenses—
but still, they got their standards."

"I have other items, ma'am. I have another white shirt
and two more sets of essential, um, underthings. I have
soap, a hairbrush and a toothbrush, an extra pair of knee
socks, paper and pens, ribbons for my hair, needles and
pins, and, you know, some private personal care items."
I knew I was blushing.

"Yeah, that's what I was afraid of." She squinted at me,
hard. "It's like you're straight out of Dickens."

I adored Charles Dickens and all his splendid novels.
"Thank you, ma'am."

My landlady rolled her eyes. "You got to quit ma'aming
all over the place. Makes me feel old. Call me Grady."

I had another piece of toast, and Grady lit another cigarette. Her lipstick was shocking pink today. She kept eyeing
my uniform. "Look, you said you want a job in one of the
cafés, right?"

I nodded.

"Well, you're a bright thing, so you must have noticed
that people here dress a little different."

I nodded again, remembering my depot savior and the
ladies in the subway. "Oh yes, it's quite wonderful! Like
what you're wearing." Grady had on a pale-blue taffeta
shirtdress with a wide, shiny black belt cinched in tight at
the waist.

"Thank you," she said, smoothing the skirt. "It's practically couture."

I nodded again. I didn't understand half the things these city people said.

"Look, sweetie, I know your money has got to be tight and all, but you're not going to get a job in the Purple Onion looking like an underage Quaker. Do you sew?"

I shook my head. Dot and Sara and Tess were the ones who sewed, and Dot had real talent. Where was she now? Where were Betty and Malou and…? My eyes stung.

Wait, what was the Purple Onion?

"Oh hey, I didn't mean to hurt your feelings!" She swept over to me. "Here, have a cigarette. It's impossible to smoke and cry at the same time, and that's a fact."

"Uh, thank you, no. I'm fine, really." I was blinking furiously to hold back the waterworks. "I used to pretend to smoke with a couple of the others in the toolshed. Maybe we all pretended. Maybe we all went back to the house and quietly threw up. No more pretending."

Grady looked completely confused.

"Thing is, I can't sew, ma'am, but I can cook and I can serve. At dinner I'd see to over thirty people by myself." I was still trying to get back on my feet after that sneak attack of homesickness. "What's the Purple Onion, if you don't mind my asking?"

"Why, it's the best club in town. Big Bob's place." She smiled then. "Even Ian Tyson comes in on occasion."

"Ian Tyson! For real?"

Crisis averted, she sat back down. "You've heard of him?"

"Yes, ma'am. I know practically everything about music. It's deep in my blood, you know?"

"Grady," she reminded me. "Well, there's hope for you yet." She stubbed out her cigarette with extra thoughtfulness. "Okay, come on. We're going to Honest Ed's. It's anything but couture, but we'll get you something that will get you in the door when the Purple Onion opens this afternoon. Bring at least twenty dollars. You need clothes, shoes and definitely some lipstick."

The Toronto bus terminal had nothing on the chaos in the monster-sized *Emporium of Everything* that was Honest Ed's. The outside, a full city block long, was smothered in neon lights and signage that beamed, *This way, you lucky people!* The inside was more like a carnival than a store. There were stairs that led nowhere, and tables overflowing with stockpots and men's undershirts side by each. Bright hand-painted signs yelled in every direction. *Don't just stand there. Buy something!!! Ed's hot deals on heaters! There's no business like shoe business!!* And, alarmingly, *Free 12 pack of baby raccoons for every visitor!*

"Relax, kid—it's a joke," said Grady as she pulled me through the maze of aisles.

Everyone from everywhere in the world was in that store, and they shouted at each other in a thousand different languages.

I loved it! There was a rhythm to the chaos that was pure music. Grady made me try on dresses and pants and skirts.

Sometimes, when a curtained cubicle was free I'd go in there to change, but most of the time I just put stuff on over Peggy's uniform. I spent more than fifteen dollars. I bought a genius skirt that was actually reversible. It was black with white checks on one side, and white with black polka dots on the other! I also bought a pair of yellow slacks with a matching cable-knit cardigan and two black turtleneck tops, one with sleeves and one without. I was relieved to buy a pair of white Keds sneakers and black ballerina flats. No more of Peggy's monster shoes for me. I also got hairbands and tights, a white purse that slung over my shoulder and, because Grady insisted I purchase them even though I didn't really need them, a brassiere and six pairs of pink underthings. They were six for sixty-six cents! And oh yeah, I bought a Maybelline lipstick and some food too.

After we got home, I changed into my brand-new clothes and made myself a sandwich. Grady pulled my hair back into a very high and tight ponytail. I couldn't stop looking at myself. When Grady came back from getting herself a "refreshment," she pronounced me perfect.

"Okay, kid, you're ready. Now go earn some money."

"How can I ever begin to thank—"

"Ah, save it!" She dismissed me with a wave. "Straight to the Onion, hear? I just want to make sure you can come up with the rent, is all. And be sure to take your Orphan Annie ID with you, in case they don't believe you're sixteen."

The Purple Onion was on the corner of Avenue Road and Yorkville Avenue, just a couple of blocks down from Grady's. Doors opened at noon and it was already past that, but I stood examining the playbill out front as if my life depended on it. Every night but Sundays and Mondays, there was a one-dollar cover charge from 8:00 PM on. The featured players were the "renowned" blues and honky-tonk band the Ramblers, featuring Brooks Goldman.

Even more arresting was a large black-and-white photo of the most handsome man that I had ever seen. *IAN TYSON ONE NIGHT ONLY AND ONLY HERE!* The date was two weeks from now.

So that was Ian Tyson. Wow. I couldn't stop looking at him. My heart rate quickened. There was something… familiar. He looked…well, actually, he kind of looked like me, or at least what I would look like if I were a grown man. Wait. Exact same mouth, same eyes, same coloring, dark hair, light blue eyes. My heart raced. Maybe the Seven weren't all loony, playing those daft games about our potential parents. Maybe…

He would be the right age…

No.

But I had that playbill featuring a band that was playing at a club called Willa's. It would make perfect sense that my father was a musician. A rover. These things happened… the Seven said that it happened all the time…

No. That was ridiculous.

But then again, where had I gotten my love of music?

The door opened and a tall skinny guy stuck his head out. Even though he was all elbows and knees, he was also undeniably cute.

"You gonna gawk at Tyson forever, or are you coming in to apply for the waitress job?"

I reddened instantly and decided to hate him. Besides, did he count as a man, therefore not to be spoken to? No, he was a boy, an older boy, not a...well, when exactly did a boy become a man? I decided to ignore Mrs. Hazelton's man rules from here on in; otherwise, the whole city would be full of people I couldn't talk to. "How did you know? I mean, yes, I want to apply, but how—"

"The Lady Grady called Big Bob and yanked his chain. I'm Ethan. You coming in, or do you want to keep swooning?"

"I most certainly was not swooning. Or gawking, for that matter."

He ignored me. Still, he *was* cute.

I followed the boy into the darkness inside. When my eyes adjusted, it was to mismatched wrought iron tables, chairs, loveseats and a small stage. "Hey, Big Bob, she's here. I found her outside panting over Tyson's picture."

Absolutely, totally hated him.

Big Bob topped out at about maybe five foot two, but he was the most tightly woven, muscular man I had ever seen anywhere. He wore a bright-white T-shirt that looked like it was straining to stay on. He'd surely bust out of it if he inhaled too deeply.

"Hey, you Orphan Annie?" Light glinted off one of his teeth. It was gold. And then there were his massive arms, which were blanketed with tattoos. I honestly didn't know where to look.

"Toni, sir. Toni Royce. Pleased to meet you." The Royce part still crawled out of my mouth all wrong, despite my practicing it in my room. I held out my hand.

The annoying boy didn't quite stifle a groan.

"The Lady Grady said you got real manners." Big Bob's hand swallowed mine. "Might be a nice change around here."

He quizzed me for several minutes and then walked me around the place, pointing out storage and showing me the kitchen, such as it was. Apparently, the Purple Onion was not renowned as a dining establishment. A couple of sandwich options and some baked goods were on offer. They served cappuccinos and espresso though. Whatever that was. A machine that came all the way over from Italy was required.

Big Bob pronounced with considerable pride that he ran a "clean place," just as I was thinking that if I got the job, I'd have to come early and clean it up proper. "And I'm shorthanded. Baby Goldman here has been helping me out for the past week or so, even though he's supposed to be tending to his dad's band."

So, the annoying boy was Ethan Goldman?

"I had to can Sandra for getting high on the job, and Rachel ran off with a trumpet player down in Gerrard Village two days ago."

Gerrard Village? That's where the club on my playbill was!

Big Bob shook his head in disbelief. "And he's bad news, man. He can't blow for beans! She always comes crawling back." More head shaking, with Ethan joining in. "I hear he has a monster habit, so she'll be tapped out in a month, ya dig?"

What *was* he talking about? "I'm sure you're right, sir. Uh, the Gerrard Village—has Mr. Tyson ever played there? A long, long time ago perhaps?"

Ethan snorted, but Big Bob seemed to consider this seriously. "Possibly. Sure, now it's pretty sketchy, but Gerrard used to be it, man. It *was* the scene in the forties and fifties. Tyson's from out west, you know. But if he came this way to do his thing, it would have been there for sure."

Bingo. Everything was lining up. It must be a sign. For sure.

"You can ask him yourself in a couple of weeks." He smiled at me, flashing his tooth.

"Does that mean that I...?"

"You start this afternoon. Ethan will show you the ropes. Six shifts a week, six hours a shift, except for one short shift, and all the tips are yours. Anyone touches you, including little Goldman here, just holler. I run a clean place. Come back at three thirty, and we'll get you started."

"Yes, sir! Thank you so much, sir!" I pretty much flew out of the place. I couldn't wait to tell Grady, to thank Grady. Oh, if only the others could see me now. My first full day in Toronto, and I had a place to live, new clothes, a brand-new job in the most exciting place in the world and…I'd already figured out who my father was!

The new me was amazing.

"Wishin' and Hopin'"

(DUSTY SPRINGFIELD)

I THOUGHT SHE was dead. I mean, who wouldn't?

I had run from the Purple Onion all the way to 75 Hazelton and, like an idiot, just burst into Grady's front parlor with my great news. That's the kind of thing that always got me into trouble back home. Grady was slumped over awkwardly in a big flower-patterned wingback chair. Her refreshment glass and a lit cigarette in an ashtray sat on a dainty side table.

"Grady! Mrs. Vespucci! Grady, are you okay?" I tried to prop her up. She wouldn't stay propped, but she did moan like she was in god-awful pain. I raced to the kitchen and grabbed the first tea towel I saw, ran it under cold water and then roared right back to her. I was patting her face with the damp cloth, pleading for her to live, when I heard someone coming down the stairs.

"Help, help, please! Mrs. Vespucci is dying!"

An elderly man with an armload of books stepped in and then hesitated.

"Please help. Mrs. Vespucci has collapsed!" Grady groaned as if to underscore the point.

The man shook his head and sighed. "You're the new tenant on the third floor?"

"Yes, sir, Toni Royce. Pleased to meet you." I said it automatically. Years of training kick in even during a crisis. I kept mopping her face as if that would bring her back to life, but it looked like most of her face was coming off on the cloth.

"Professor Edward Zeigler at your service, Miss Toni Royce. I have rooms on the second floor." He actually bowed his head. "I shouldn't overly concern yourself, Miss Royce. The Lady Grady is not dying—she's passed out."

"Passed out! But, sir, that could be grievous!"

More head shaking. "No, I don't think you fully comprehend the situation. It's a condition"—he paused—"a condition that both she and I find ourselves in a bit too often. She's plastered."

Again with the words. Why couldn't anyone speak plain English?

He stepped closer to us. "The Lady Grady is inebriated—drunk—my dear. Very, very drunk."

I stopped dabbing at her face. "The refreshments?"

"The..." He cleared his throat. "Yes, Grady tends to refresh with bourbon—that's a spirit, my dear. It's a leftover from one of her husbands, the American one, I believe. I prefer the more poetic demon rum. She'll sleep it off."

He'd lost me again. What did spirits have to do with nationality? Wait, did he say *husbands*? Plural?

"Well, if you'll excuse me, I have a class to bore."

And I had to get to work. "But she'll be okay—after the sleeping off, I mean?"

"As right as rain. Well, perhaps a headache. You look like a reader. I'll drop off some books at your door from time to time. Lovely to make your acquaintance." And he was off.

Okay then.

I looked around the room and spotted an ottoman, and I dragged it over to Grady's chair to put her feet up. She muttered something as I removed her shiny black high heels. Much to my awe, her toenails were painted the exact same shade as her fingernails. How shocking and beautiful! Unfortunately, a large ugly bump on the side of each big toe disfigured what would have been very pretty feet. I'm deeply ashamed to admit that I longed to slip on those splendid shoes. Instead, I propped her up as best I could and then covered her with a sofa blanket. After washing out the tea towel, which was soiled with makeup, I threw out her refreshment and refilled the glass with water. *Drunk, just drunk.* I watched her breathe until just before 3:30 PM, when I tore back to the Purple Onion in time for my very first shift.

I felt years older and infinitely wiser than when I had first walked through those doors a couple of hours ago. Imagine a lady getting *drunk!*

Predictably, Ethan was annoying for that shift and pretty much every shift thereafter. He was mainly annoying because he was such a know-it-all, even though he was only nineteen. This was made much worse by the fact that he really did seem to know a lot, and it was becoming clearer by the minute that I pretty much knew nothing. I had always, and not so secretly, thought of myself as the smart one at the orphanage. I *hated* feeling stupid.

Still, little by little I got better at city language. When things were good or fun, they were a "gas," a "blast," "cool," or "boss." When Big Bob wanted me to relax, he'd tell me to "hang loose" or "go with the flow." All in all, it was easier than French, but there was just so much of it. By the end of the first week, I not only knew the difference between a cappuccino and an espresso, but I was the best at making them. The patrons were occasionally rambunctious, but for the most part they were happy just to "hang out" and listen to Mr. Goldman's band, which was "cool." I had already written to Joe about everything. Well, not about Grady passing out, but pretty much everything else. I'd barely seen Grady since that day. She seemed to make herself scarce even when I came down with the rent.

Perhaps I had given offense by presuming to take her shoes off.

I also started several letters to Betty but never finished one. Someday soon, I would write Betty and tell her all my news. I would write about meeting my father. This, I kept telling myself, was completely different from all the silly fantasizing back at the orphanage. This wasn't *wishin' and hopin'* nonsense; this was real.

Betty would forgive me for my gutless departure. Betty always forgave me. God, I missed her.

There were moments when Ethan and I got along. He did have the most wonderful chocolate-brown eyes, and his mouth was...well, if he weren't so angular, it would come dangerously close to being lovely. Despite having worked in and around his father's band since he was a toddler, Ethan wanted to be lawyer. He fancied himself intelligent, and, okay, maybe he kind of was. The day before Ian Tyson's gig, I made the mistake of asking him if Mr. Tyson would come in early to rehearse, the way I'd seen Ethan's father's band do when they tried out new material. And he changed on me again.

"Why? You looking to throw yourself at him before the rest of the chicks?"

"No! Ewww!"

"You want to marry him. All the girls who come want to marry him, or..." His dark eyes got darker still. "But he's going to marry Sylvia, so a bit of a glitch, huh?"

I felt like the top of my head was going to explode. "I certainly do *not* want to marry him! That would be highly inappropriate, and against the laws of man and nature."

Oops.

"Huh?" He stopped washing the countertop. Ever since I'd started working there, I'd been going hard on a cleanup campaign, and Ethan grudgingly went along. "What? Why? What do you mean?"

Now what?

"You must absolutely swear to secrecy."

"Sure."

I'd gone way too far, but there was no backing down. Besides, Ethan knew so much, he might prove helpful. "I, uh, so…I believe that there is some chance, maybe, that Mr. Ian Tyson is my natural father. Actually, all the facts point to it."

He looked at me like I had two heads. "Okay, that's even stupider than I expected."

"Is not!"

"Is too!" He snorted. "Is this, like, an orphan thing, like a movie in your head?"

And there it was. He'd pricked my soft spot. I felt like a furnace. How dare he? If he only knew that *I* was the one who had never, ever allowed herself to indulge in all that ridiculousness. *I* was the one with her feet planted firmly into seriously unwanted reality when it came to that stuff. The best I could come up with was "Is not!" I lost all our arguments. I hated that. But what I hated more was being called stupid, because deep, deep down I worried that it might be true. "And what's really stupid is your name. What kind name is Ethan?"

"Well, in my case, it's Jewish. You got something against Jews?"

Okay, he had me there. I had to think about it. "I don't think so. Am I supposed to? I don't know any Jewish-type people."

"Well, you do now. What have you got against me? I'm busting my butt showing you the ropes, cleaning stuff with vinegar nonstop, and you ignore me unless you need instant Tyson info."

"I do not!"

"You do so, and you're acting real stupid to boot!"

And there it was again. "That's only because you make me feel stupid, and you—you're awful!"

That's when he should have apologized for a whole bunch of things, but mainly for making me feel so... well, whatever that was. I folded my arms and waited for the apology. I would take my own sweet time in carefully considering said apology.

But all he said was, "Awful? I'm awful?" Then he dropped the rag and walked away.

Fine. Who cared? Not me. I filled up the sugar canisters, the salt and pepper shakers, the vinegar and ketchup bottles. It took me right up until opening. Ethan stayed clear of me the rest of the night. Like I said, fine. The next night I would meet my father and Ethan would see...Ian Tyson would know as soon as he took one look at me. Big Bob and Mr. Goldman and the band would cheer as my father took me in his arms. The crowd would go wild. *Movie in my head* my foot! What did Ethan know?

I only hoped that I could learn to love my new stepmother.

"Someday Soon"

(IAN AND SYLVIA)

GRADY WAS ACTUALLY coming to the club! She wanted to see Ian Tyson. It seemed that she had forgiven me for taking off her shoes and/or seeing her overly refreshed that one time. I'd been babbling about him all afternoon. She called me down after lunch to assess her wardrobe selection. "So what do you think, kid? You're not much, but you're all I've got." She twirled around in a red-satin, full-skirted dress with a plunging neckline. Ruby earrings that practically came down to her shoulders. They almost, but not quite, distracted you from her significant chest area. People just did not look like that in the Purple Onion. Actually, people did not look like that anywhere.

"You look like a blond Elizabeth Taylor!" At the orphanage, we were allowed to watch television only one night a week unless there was an Elizabeth Taylor or Audrey Hepburn movie on. Then we got extra time. Miss Webster was partial to them.

"Exactly what I was going for!" She gave her hair an extra shot of spray. "I have a reputation to maintain." More energetic spritzing. "When the Lady Grady goes out, people expect Hollywood, and that's what I give 'em." She eyed me as she lit a cigarette. "Red lips, Toni. Tonight you gotta have red lips. Here!" She proffered a golden tube. "Fire and Ice will be perfect with your coloring."

Red lips? Red lips were for movie stars and fast women and ladies like Grady. I could never—what if Mrs. Hazelton saw? Of course, that last thought made me consider it in a new light. "Sure, if you're sure."

"Am I sure! I know what's best for you, don't I? Didn't I get you the job?"

I nodded.

"Red lips it is," Grady said. It was a shockingly laborious process. A lip brush, Kleenex, powder and multiple "blottings" were involved. "Gorgeous! Your lips are a little large, but I think that's coming into fashion soon."

It had better be immediate. All I could see was my lips. It was like the rest of me had left the room. I honestly couldn't say what I thought of myself, whether I was better or worse, but I was definitely noticeable. It kind of shook me up. We admired ourselves tremendously in the mirror. Grady sighed a lot, which made me worry a bit about how many refreshments she had already partaken of.

"Gotta go!" I needed to take myself and my big red lips to the club.

"Okay, doll, I'll see ya later. Just don't drink or eat anything. You don't know how to do it without messing up your mouth."

"Yes, ma'am, thank you."

As I closed the front door, I heard: "And don't *ma'am* me, damn it."

I fretted the whole way to work that Mr. Tyson's ability to recognize me as his long-lost daughter would be somehow hampered by the liberal application of Fire and Ice.

"Whoa, what happened to you?" Ethan stopped in his tracks.

"Huh?"

"You look like you got punched in the mouth."

Hated him did not begin to cover it.

"Hey, Toni, thanks for coming in early," Big Bob said. "It's going to be a big night. Whoo-ee baby!" He was grinning from ear to ear, and his gold tooth gleamed under the stage lights. I could smell cologne wafting off him. It looked like he had broken out a brand-new T-shirt in honor of the occasion. All this for Ian Tyson? "Girl, you look fine!"

Ethan rolled his eyes before loping off.

"Thank you, uh…" I always got stuck at this part. Calling my employer by his Christian name seemed disrespectful in the extreme, and besides, what, technically, *was* his first name? Big or Bob? Ethan called him "Big Guy," but they were practically family. "Thank you," I repeated.

The place filled up fast. By eight thirty, a full half hour before Mr. Tyson's set, every table except for the little one closest to the stage was occupied. Apparently, I had just missed the warmup with the Ramblers by minutes, and Mr. Tyson was sequestered with Ethan's father backstage. I was hopping so fast that I didn't have time to be disappointed. Just before 9:00 PM, a ripple of whispers rode through the Onion, directed at the entrance. Was Mr. Tyson going to come in from the front rather than from backstage?

No.

It was Grady.

She paused at the doorway, in all her glorious, high-heeled, plunging-necklined, satin best. My employer shot over before she could take another step. Big Bob was a pretty happy kind of guy, all in all, but now he was pulsing like a strobe light. The cologne, the new T-shirt. Grady? Big Bob and Grady? I was hustling to deliver the last round of cappuccinos before the set, but Grady stopped and made sure she caught my eye before she waved her fingers at me. The whole room turned, and it looked like no one had ever seen me in the place before. Only then did she swan in on the tattooed arm of Big Bob, who looked like he was going to bust a kidney. Who was this woman? Clearly, there was more to my landlady than met the eye, and that was saying something.

Big Bob beckoned me over and whispered, "Two double espressos, fast." I raced over to the coffee bar, steamrolled over Ethan, who was working the machine, and raced back with their drinks just as Brooks Goldman started his intro.

"Only right here! Only right now! Let's hear it for the mighty Ian Tyson!"

The applause and whistling was deafening. Women clasped their hands to their chests. Men thumped the tables. He didn't have to do anything but walk up to the mic and he had everyone with a pulse in the palm of his hands. My heart lurched. That was my father. *My father.* I may have whispered that a few times. He was so incredibly...Grady grabbed my arm. "Quit licking your lips. You won't have anything left by the end of the set!"

My father was an imposingly handsome man. I somehow made my way back to the coffee bar, tried not to gawk and did not succeed. I could feel Ethan's death stare on my back the whole time. As soon as the applause and thumping died down, Tyson launched into "Someday Soon." What a voice! There was a bittersweet, lonely catch in it that went straight to my bone marrow. What was I doing? Talent like that should not be shackled by a love child. Though I did love the sound of those two words, *love child.* But a lot was riding on this, more than the obvious. Thing is, if someone as gloriously stupendous as Mr. Ian Tyson could fall in love with my monster mom, maybe she wasn't such a monster after all.

The joint was jumpin' the whole night. In between sets, Ethan and I and even Big Bob had to spring into action. Ethan managed to spit out that he didn't buy for a minute that I thought Ian Tyson was my father. "Nobody moons over their dad like you've been mooning over him all night! You're just like all the other girls."

I spat right back that he should get his head out of the gutter. I wasn't 100 percent sure what that meant, but I'd heard it used by some of our female patrons, and it seemed to suit the occasion.

Mr. Tyson closed the second set with Brooks Goldman singing harmony to "Four Strong Winds," which is, bar none, the most perfect song ever written. That catch, deep in the basement of his throat, made the song lonelier, lovelier. It was hard not to cry. I couldn't have been prouder of my father. The club went wild. Everyone got on their feet and tried to converge around Mr. Tyson, but he made his way straight over to Grady's table and kissed her hand.

Really, who the heck was this woman?

I fought my way into the crowd surrounding the table. I wasn't going to declare myself in front of all these people—I'd been raised better—but I could at least meet him and see if I could get in a word alone later. My heart was hammering so loud it drowned out the noise of the crowd. Grady had just said something to make both Mr. Tyson and Big Bob laugh, and then she saw me.

"Ian, honey, I'd like to introduce you to Toni. Toni lives with me."

Mr. Tyson actually stood up, reached for my hand and kissed it. Somehow, I stayed standing. I'd already stopped breathing at the "Ian, honey" part.

"I noticed you the minute I hit the stage, darling." He winked at me. "Sit down, sweet thing, I'd love to buy you"—small, brilliant, killer half smile—"a cuppa coffee."

"Well, my!" Grady smoothed out the satin folds of her dress. "Look at the time!" Grady wasn't wearing a watch—never did, never would. "Sorry, boys. Toni and I need our beauty sleep." This was met with outrage and groans from the assembled throng, and confusion on my part. I still had cleanup. "You don't mind if Toni walks me home, do you, Bobby?"

Bobby?

Big Bob flashed his gold tooth. "'Course not. Anything for my Lady Grady. She came in early. Ethan and I will close up." Big Bob stood up and helped her out of her chair.

Wait! What? The tables were a mess, and I had to stay and tell Mr. Tyson about us, about him and me and, well, I guess my mother had to figure in there somewhere. God knew when he'd be back, what with his wedding and all. Maybe I should have told Grady all about it, but then I remembered Ethan's ridiculous reaction. No, it was my secret, or I was his secret—but I couldn't be his secret if he didn't know I was his secret, could I? I was making myself dizzy.

Grady took my arm and led us straight out of the place, knowing that every eye was trained on her.

What would that feel like?

As soon as we hit Hazelton, I started to whine. "Thing is, I should have stayed, Grady. I really needed to talk to Mr. Tyson about something important." She snorted and held my arm tighter. "No, really," I said. "I was hoping to see him after I cleaned up."

"Yeah, he was hoping plenty too." We had to stop so she could light a cigarette.

Oh my god! Had Mr. Tyson deduced that I was his child just by looking at me? He did say he had noticed me right away. Things like that happened all the time in the Bible and in the movies, and now Grady had ruined everything. When was I ever going to see him again? "It was, like, really, critically important, Grady."

She blew smoke in my face. "I knew you'd be trouble the moment I saw you, Orphan Annie. You plopped yourself down in the middle of the city straight from a two-bit town, and an orphanage at that. You might as well have come in from another century. Honey, you don't even know the things you don't know."

"You sound just like Joe and the matron!" I may have been pouting. I don't pout well, no matter how hard I try.

"Ha! Well, that's rich. A matron. That's one for the ages. Step on it—I need a refreshment." She put her arm through mine again. "Look, honey, the man's a tomcat. Sylvia is buying herself a world of hurt."

Of course, I didn't have a clue what she was going on about, or what my future stepmother had to do with anything. I replayed every detail from the introduction on. My head reeled through the conversation, the pauses, the looks, every little gesture. It wasn't until we got to 75 Hazelton that I almost tripped on it. Wait a gosh-darned minute! Back there, at the club, had my father actually winked at me?

"I Get Around"

(THE BEACH BOYS)

THE NIGHTMARES WERE back. The new me, the *real* me, would no longer have nightmares. That was the deal. I made this pledge every night for almost a month before going to bed. And it worked, until it didn't. By July the nightmares found my new address and slid in with the heat. The fire, the shattered glass piercing me, the blood, the screaming. And worst of all…my mother hurting me. I must have been screaming, because the pounding on my door woke me up. It was the professor.

"Miss Royce, are you okay? Miss Royce! Toni, please answer."

I was disoriented as I felt my way to the door. The professor looked moderately disoriented himself. He swayed as he gripped his glass. He apologized for his condition as soon as I opened the door.

"No, sir, please. I should be the one to apologize. It's the dreams. I haven't had one since I came to Toronto. I thought

I left them back at the orphanage. My friends, they knew…"
And at the mere mention of them my lip started to quiver,
whether from missing them or the shame of the dreams I
couldn't be sure. "I am very, very sorry to have disturbed you, sir."

"Oh dear, Miss Royce. Well, I am certainly in no position
to give anyone life advice. However"—he leaned against the
doorjamb to steady himself—"may I gently suggest that you
find the source of your demons before your demons over-
take you. Perhaps you need to find some answers."

"Yes, sir." I was snuffling. "I will, sir." Was that it? I had to
get to the bottom of it all? What was the bottom? I couldn't
count on the professor continuing to be as understanding
about my midnight screams as Betty and the others had
been. "I promise, and I apologize again for disturbing your
evening."

"Not at all, Miss Royce." He took a sip from his glass.
"Sweet dreams."

Not likely. I was afraid to go back to bed. I turned Joe's
little transistor on real low and listened to CHUM 1050
right up until I thought I heard Grady stirring downstairs.
I also started and stopped a hundred letters to Betty. When
the Beach Boys came on at 9:05 AM with "I Get Around,"
I got up to visit Grady.

I knocked on the parlor door.

Oh my…

"What's the matter? Never seen anyone hung over
before?" She tightened the sash on her silk robe. "What am
I saying?" She snorted. "I keep forgetting you're greener

than grass." Grady's hands shook as she lit a cigarette. Her lipstick was smeared. Her hair was stuck flat against the left side of her head but seemed to be trying to make a break for it from the right.

"You're ill! You shouldn't be up." I took her by the arm and led her to her favorite armchair. "I'm going to make you some tea and toast and set you right!"

"Geez, kid, are they all like you in that little twinkle town of yours? I'm just hungover. Eddy and I got into the sauce pretty good last night. Thing is, I pass out but I can't sleep. You know?"

Of course, I didn't. "Eddy?"

"Professor Zeigler. Even though he can outdrink me, I'm a bad influence on him. I'm a bad influence on everyone." She sighed and stubbed out her cigarette. "But I won't say no to tea, toast and aspirins. They're in the cupboard above the sink." She burrowed into the chair and put her feet up on the ottoman.

I started fixing things in the kitchen. What was wrong with this woman? Grady was clearly a major glamorous somebody, but she kept refreshing herself into a stupor. Mrs. Hazelton would have set her straight in a flash.

I, on the other hand, was flummoxed. She was the adult, after all. Adults were another species, all-knowing and all-powerful. I may have rebelled against that at the orphanage, but it was safe to do so there. The rules were clear.

When I returned with the tray, Grady was smearing white goop on her face and wiping it off with tissues.

"Never use soap and water, kid. Ruins the complexion. I'll get you some of this." She lifted the jar—Pond's Cold Cream. "I got a source. It's practically free."

"Thank you. Uh, I was hoping we could talk a bit."

"Sure, kid. Take a load off." She moved her feet over so I could sit on the ottoman. She dry-swallowed four aspirins before picking up her teacup. "Shoot."

"Well, do you remember the other night at the Purple Onion?" Grady smiled. She actually looked more girlish without all of her fancy makeup on. "Mr. Tyson…"

"Listen up, Toni, you don't even know what a hangover is. How do you think you could possibly have handled Ian Tyson?"

"Handled?"

"I'm assuming you're a virgin?"

"What?" I just about fell off the ottoman. "Of course I am!"

"Ever been kissed?"

Okay, I'd been dreaming about getting kissed since forever—longer, even. I examined the floor.

"Thought so, and here you have one of the country's biggest playboys gunning for your shorts. Honey, you wouldn't have stood a chance, you and your little romantic dreams."

"Romantic dreams? Gunning for me, like he wanted to…? No! Eeeww! He wouldn't! He couldn't! Mr. Tyson is my father!"

"What the…?" The toast dropped onto the plate, and Grady reached for a cigarette. "Why in God's name would you think that?"

I stood up. "Well, there's the music thing. I got music in my bones, except I don't have any real aptitude for it, but you know my radio's on all the time, and there is an undeniably strong resemblance, except maybe he's actually prettier than I am, and the age is right, and I have this playbill, and Big Bob said that if Mr. Tyson were in Toronto in the late forties, well, he'd have gone to Gerrard Village, and I think the age works, and did you see his eyes? They're just like my eyes, and not only that but the hair too, and did I mention the Willa's playbill, and—"

"Take a breath! You're turning purple."

I gulped some air.

"Ian wasn't playing the Toronto clubs back then." She shook her head. "Honey, he was out west. He didn't come out here once in the forties. I'm sorry, kid. He may be the daddy to a lot of little girls for all I know, but he's not your daddy."

But it was all so perfect.

I sat down with a thump. I had been so certain. It all fit...but, of course, it didn't. I had done *that* thing, the orphan thing, talked myself right into a fantasy. Was the need that big? Even in the cold-water shower shock, I saw it for was it was. And here I'd been mocking the others. I'd even read up on Sylvia in the magazines. I was pretty sure we would have gotten along.

Was the *new* me, the *real* me, an idiot?

"And what got into your head about Gerrard Village and your daddy anyways?"

Well, in for a penny…"I'll be right back." I took the stairs two at a time, unearthed my precious but pathetic clues and raced back down with the playbill.

"This is one of the only clues I have about who I am, see."

Grady held the purple playbill at arm's length and squinted at it. "Yeah, Willa's was in the Village, all right, but it is no more. My second husband owned a lot of those clubs. Not that one, but a lot of them. I see where you got the idea your dad's a musician though."

I was still licking my wounds over Mr. Tyson, but my curiosity about Grady momentarily trumped my disappointment. "Second husband? Uh, how many…?" I cleared my throat.

"Four, but who's counting? Like I said, I'm a bad influence." It looked like she was going to say something, then changed her mind. "I need a refreshment."

"But it's only ten thirty," I called after her.

"Hair of the dog, kid."

What? But Grady came back brandishing a tall glass of tomato juice, so I relaxed.

"I never paid much attention to my husband's club scene in those days," she said, settling back into the chair. "I was too busy restarting my film career. Ha!" She rolled her head back in the chair on the *ha*.

"Grady, it's important. It could be that my father—okay, not Mr. Tyson, I see that now—but I bet my *real* father played there or worked there or was there, you see? All I've got is this playbill, my hospital-release form and a restaurant menu. It's a real clue, Grady."

She took a gulp of her tomato juice and softened. "Sure, I can see how you'd think so. But Gerrard Village doesn't exist anymore. It's just a bunch of seedy bars, users, hookers and players. No place for you to go poking around. It would make Tyson look like a walk in the park."

She had lost me again.

Grady took another gulp. She must've been dehydrated from the hangover thing.

"You know who might know? Brooks! Brooks was into the scene in the late forties. He was just coming up, but he would been around those clubs." She was nodding to herself. "Yup, Ethan was a baby and Brooks was scrambling for gigs. It pissed off his old lady, Janice, something fierce until she came right around and then..." She shrugged. "You know Brooks is actually a lawyer?"

Two things hit me at once. Maybe that was why Ethan wanted to be a lawyer, and, much more important, the coloring was *exactly* right. Not Ethan's, Mr. Goldman's.

"Actually, Janice stepped up big-time. Looking back, it couldn't have been easy. She had this kid and, poor thing, she marries a lawyer and ends up with a musician, you know?"

He was the right age. Sure, his hair was gray now, but you could tell it must have been brown, and the eyes were right. Bright blue. Ethan was dark—dark eyes, dark skin, dark hair. He must take after his mother.

"But man, she hounded him at the start."

Hmm...Troubled marriage. I'd read about this kind of thing in the *True Romance* magazines Tess had sneaked into the orphanage. It happened all the time in your big cities.

Mr. Goldman must have played at Willa's.

"So talk to him."

She was nodding. "Yeah, Brooks might have something for you."

He'd been real nice to me right off the bat, fatherly-like. Mr. Goldman? Yes? No? Maybe. I argued with myself as I stood there until I wore myself out. It was an intense exchange. It made way more sense than the whole Ian Tyson thing, after all.

But wait. Would that make Ethan my stepbrother? Or, worse, my half brother?

"Yeah." Grady nodded dreamily. "Brooks knew the scene back then. Hell, he *was* the scene." She drained her glass and looked much comforted until she saw the look on my face. "What is it?"

I couldn't tell her about my hunch. It was too new, still brewing. They were friends, after all. I needed more information. I was going to be sensible this time. Yup. Wait. Wait! Did this mean...?

Holy mother of God, I was Jewish!

"Bits and Pieces"

(THE DAVE CLARK FIVE)

OF COURSE, I looked at Ethan in a whole new light. A very uncomfortable one. I mean, he was my brother, and I had all these confusing feelings that were, um, confusing. Since the very beginning, I'd gotten this kind of panicky, fluttery feeling in my stomach whenever he came near me. It must be a long-lost-sibling type of reaction. Or something.

I avoided him for the next two shifts.

This was relatively easy because it seemed that he was busy avoiding me. It was like we were in a contest.

Who cared? Not me.

I got busy obsessing about where I could buy a Star of David. Did Jewish churches sell them? It wouldn't be big or gaudy, just a discreet little one that I would wear all the time to help me connect to my people. Maybe the pawnshops would have one. I also pledged to go to the Yorkville Library and read up on my new faith. But all that would have to wait until I found out more about my immediate family. If Mr. Goldman was my father, maybe he had met my mother in the clubs in the late forties. But I couldn't very well ask him. I promised myself that I wasn't going to go all Tyson on him, not even in my head. I needed hard evidence before I tackled my potential father. That left Big Bob.

I came in an hour early on Wednesday afternoon and tracked him down in the storage room.

"Hey, what's up?" He was moving sacks of coffee beans from one pile to another. Was he exercising? Maybe the beans needed jiggling.

"Uh, could we talk, uh…"

"Call me Bob. You get all tortured-looking when I see you fumbling around for a name."

I must have looked stricken.

"Okay, Big Bob then. You can do it. Look, I know they must have had crazy-ass rules about manners at the asylum…"

"Orphanage."

"Orphanage." He nodded. "But a coffeehouse is a different species, toots. Even some of the customers have seen you choke when you want to get my attention."

"I'm sorry, uh, Big, um, Bob."

"It'll get easier." He sighed. "So what do you want to talk to me about?" He dropped a sack at his feet. "Is Grady okay?"

"Grady?"

"She's not drinking too much, is she?"

Grady tended to over-refresh most days, sometimes with the professor but usually alone. Today, however, she had been clear-eyed and drinking coffee when I came down to say goodbye, so I went with that. "She was just great when I left her."

He flashed his tooth at that. "So what is it? You need to get off early?"

"No, sir, Big Bob." I grabbed a sack of beans from one pile and threw it onto the other. "The thing is, I've been sort of searching for my roots." I kept piling the sacks. They were heavy, but it made the talking easier. "And I got this clue that maybe my dad worked in a club called Willa's, in Gerrard Village, back in the day, you know?" Big Bob stopped heaving sacks. I did not. "Grady said that Willa's isn't there anymore, but I was hoping that there might be another place with staff or patrons who might have a connection to it and I could—I don't know—ask questions, find a clue…"

He took a sack out of my hands. "You've had it rougher than most. I keep forgetting that, what with your uptown manners and all. Look, give the Bohemian Embassy on St. Nicholas Street a try. It's *the* spot now, and they're good people in there. If anyplace would have any of the old crew that really knew the scene back then, it would be there. It's a cool soup of old-timers and beats."

"Beats?"

"Beatniks."

"Oh," I said. Was there, like, a dictionary somewhere for this kind of stuff? "Thanks. Maybe I'll go tonight after my shift." I must have been staring at him.

"Anything else, Toni?"

"Well, Grady…"

"Is a gem of a lady, a precious jewel. You can tell just by looking at her. Always was, always will be."

"Yes, for sure. She's been really good to me, but sometimes she seems to need to refresh a…a fair bit. I want to be understanding, but…I don't understand. I know that there have been four husbands."

Big Bob sat on his pile of coffee-bean sacks, and I followed suit on mine.

"She told you, huh?" He was nodding. "Yeah, she digs you." He crossed his massive arms, which made the tattoos flicker and twitch. "We were all kids together. Mario, her first husband, me and Grady. We were going to be unstoppable. Grady was destined for Hollywood, Mario was going be in business, and I…" He shrugged.

"Where is Mr. Vespucci now?"

"Well, that's no secret. He's in the Kingston Pen, manslaughter. Mario ended up working in his father's business sometime in the early fifties. That's when the Mafia really started making inroads in this city. He divorced her, you know."

"He did?" What kind of business organization was the Mafia? Big Bob had made a face when he said it. Was it a department store, a new bank?

"I think it's one of few decent things old buddy Mario ever did, actually."

"And the others? I mean, the other husbands."

"Well, the next one was quick. He was older and dropped dead of a heart attack in his fifties, but at least he left her 75 Hazelton and a nice cushion, you know?" Big Bob repositioned himself on the biggest pile of sacks. "Then there was Bad News Norton; he owned a pile of clubs here but came up from Detroit. He was rough on her, if you get my drift, and she finally divorced him. And then there was Philip, all good manners and elegance but made Norton look like a choirboy. He put her in the hospital a couple of times before we got rid of him."

We? Where was Big Bob in this? It was clear as glass that he was crazy about her. Why didn't *he* marry her? This was so grown up—and desperately exciting, but it made me feel like I'd been raised in a cupboard.

"Through it all, Grady quietly seeded half the clubs and shops in this village. She was better than a bank. Hollywood's loss was Yorkville's gain." He shook his head. "But it was her loss too."

"I guess that explains a lot." I didn't know what else to say. I cared about these people. But I didn't understand them. I probably didn't understand Mrs. Hazelton or Miss Webster or any of the teachers either, but things were a whole lot simpler there—their lives seemed simpler. Time to change the topic. "I'm also wondering about a whole other thing, if you don't mind. I'm researching the old jazz clubs, and I was wondering if Mr. Goldman would ever have played at Willa's."

Big Bob seemed to come back from wherever he had gone to. "Good old Willa's! Sure, Brooks had gigs there, good ones too."

My heart beat faster. That was it—bull's-eye! I didn't need anything else. But then I surprised myself by asking, "Have you ever maybe heard of a Halina Royce?"

"Halina? Halina Royce? Maybe…can't be sure. Little blond thing? Yeah, she was sort of…" He shook his head. "But there were all kinds back then. Don't know what happened to her. I think there was a kid…wait. What's it to you?"

"Her name is listed on my hospital-release form as my mother."

"Whoa, I keep tripping over the orphan part. I wish I knew more to tell you. Sorry, but I can't be any real help on that one. Lots of changes around here since then. Not that many of us old-timers left, you know."

"No, no, that's okay. Thanks, Big Bob."

"See?" He smiled.

"What?"

"Didn't that come easier?"

"Yes. Sir." I smiled. "I better start my shift."

She was kind of what, Big Bob? Insane? The kind to try to kill her child? I got a record three orders wrong that night. I could feel Ethan's disapproving eyes on me the whole night. Wouldn't he be sorry when he found out he'd been treating his sister so badly?

My shift ended at eleven, but I didn't get to the Bohemian Embassy until almost midnight. Even with Bob's directions, I got lost three times. Each time I fumbled, the area got sketchier and the streets got blacker. *It's the new me, and the new me is going to find the real me.* I whispered it as a mantra, and that sort of worked until I got the sense that someone was following me. At one point a gentleman in a red Chevy rolled down his window and yelled out, "Fifteen bucks!"

I walked faster, but he kept on right beside me. "Come on, chickie, you're not going to get a better offer!"

I stopped breathing.

Then a voice came out of the darkness. "Get lost, jerkface!"

The car took off, and so did I.

"Wait, Toni! Slow down—it's me!"

Ethan? He got to me in three strides. "Ethan, what are you doing here?"

"You're welcome, Toni." He crossed his arms. "No problem, Toni. I live to scare off johns."

"You knew his name?"

He groaned. "I keep forgetting you were raised in an incubator. A john is a...oh forget it. What are you doing here?"

"Never mind. What are *you* doing here?"

"You first."

"No, you."

"Why are you here?"

"Why are *you* here?"

Why were we always locked in mortal combat? Why was I always so uppity around him? No, wait, why was he always so uppity around me?

"I was following you. Toronto's not some sleepy little village. This is a big dangerous city, and you go waltzing off into the night. I've followed you a couple of times, especially when we've locked up really late, just to make sure you got home okay."

That stopped me cold. That he cared enough...that he...my head spun. "It's just what a big brother would do."

"Huh?"

Oh no! I'd said that out loud? Again? I'd been spending far too much time alone. I couldn't seem to keep a decent secret. Now what? Well, we were kin, after all. "Okay, so don't go all holier than thou on me, because this time isn't like the last time."

"What, Toni?"

"It'll actually make sense when you think about it."

"Toni!"

"Well, *Ethan*, I have credible evidence that you are my half brother. I believe that your father is probably my father too, and I'm just going to—"

"*What?* I've got nothing to do with Tyson!"

"No, no, no. That was absolutely ridiculous. I see that now. It was a fantasy, just like you said. Point for your side." My hands were flailing all over the place, and Ethan was tracking them. *Get a grip, Toni.* "Look, Ethan, please don't tell him yet, but I think Mr. Goldman, your dad, is my father as well, and I'm going to collect some proof at the Bohemian Embassy. People in there might remember the connections. I am your sister, Ethan—well, half sister, but you know…"

Ethan just stood there, hands on hips and mouth open. "And what kind of harebrained evidence do you have for that? There is no way that my old man stepped out on my mom, *no* way!"

"You don't have to get so heated about it." I crossed my arms to hold them still. "I think your father played at Willa's." Then I realized that this rather seminal fact would mean nothing to him. "Plus, I've got this major thing for music. My radio is on *all* the time, and there is an undeniable resemblance. You can't argue that. There is no use fighting it, Ethan. I am probably your sister." I said the last bit as gently as I could.

Instead of nodding his head thoughtfully, Ethan shoved his hands into his pockets and just up and walked away, muttering the whole time. "Let it go, Ethan, just let it go."

Okay, sure, it was a lot to take in all of a sudden. "Wait, Ethan! Where's the Bohemian Embassy?"

"You're standing in front of it, third floor." He obviously couldn't get away fast enough.

Well, all siblings have their rough patches.

"The House of the Rising Sun"

(THE ANIMALS)

WELL, WHAT A disappointment! This was the Bohemian Embassy? Shouldn't it be fancier? I had to climb up two flights of really narrow stairs that didn't even have a banister. They were dark and dingy. Just as I was going to head back down, I heard singing and then applause. It was the tail end of the Animals' big hit "The House of the Rising Sun." Joe loved that song, thought it was "all that baby, just all that."

I had to wait for my eyes to adjust when I got to the doorway. The club was even smokier than the Purple Onion, and that was saying something. Still, it got better inside. The actual room looked like the inside of a barn, but the patrons sat around tables with cheerful checkered tablecloths. Candles were stuck in wine bottles on each table. I made a mental note to talk to Big Bob about improving our decor. I scanned the room, looking for old people. I spotted a couple of "geezers," as Big Bob called them, at the table farthest from the stage. I steeled myself and made my way over.

"Good evening, gentlemen. Do you think you would mind if I joined you?"

"Sure, sugar, take a load off and brighten our table." His voice reminded me of Joe. *Joe.* It was like he was with me tonight. The man, whose name was Buddy, motioned for the waitress, who was way cooler than I was. In fact, all the waitresses were. Each and every one was beautiful, and each and every one looked bored out of their skulls. Is that why they looked so cool? I vowed to cultivate that look.

"Isn't it a little late for you to be out, young lady?" asked Buddy.

I explained that I had just come from my shift at the Purple Onion. Without any effort at all, we got to talking about the Yorkville scene versus Gerrard Village "back in the day." They both knew of Grady and Big Bob. Buddy said that after a time everybody knows everybody. I took that as my cue and asked if either of them remembered a woman named Halina Royce.

"Can't say it rings a bell," said Murphy, who had been Buddy's best friend "since God was a boy."

Buddy frowned. "Sure it does. Halina. Cute little blond number floated around Gerrard. Kind of out of it at times, but harmless. A sweet thing, ya dig?"

Kind of out of it. Didn't Big Bob say something like that?

"Oh yeah." Murphy stroked his chin with gnarled fingers. "She worked the clubs, dished drinks, cleaned, did just about anything short of the johns. I'm pretty sure she didn't roll that way. Man, she hasn't been around forever. Maybe she went back to where she came from. That'd be good. Yup."

I had gotten snagged a few sentences back.

"Uh, would you mind telling me what the *Johns* are?"

Both men looked uncomfortable. They examined their cups as if the coffee would produce the answer. "Well, the thing is, young lady..." Buddy was still staring at his cup. "That's not a topic fit for discussing with young ladies."

"Please. I really, really need to know. I can't understand half the things that you Toronto people talk about it, and this *John* word has already come up once tonight. I'm sick of feeling so stupid all the time."

"I see." Murphy cleared his throat and started stroking his chin in earnest. "Well, child, see, a man who wants to pay for the, er, company..." I nodded as if I understood. "No, that ain't right, not just the company, for the, uh, well, sexual favors of a woman who sells those, I mean her sexual favors, for a price...those men are called johns."

The room dropped away.

"You mean a prostitute? Like in the Bible, Mary Magdalene?"

"Uh, I...guess. Never heard it put quite that way." Buddy shrugged.

I blush to admit that I spent time wondering whether the fifteen dollars I had been offered by the man in the Chevy was the going rate. I mean, was I exceptional or below market?

The fellas and I talked about the old days over our coffees, which were nowhere near as good as what I made at the Purple Onion. Finally, they excused themselves.

"It pains me, but I gotta get my beauty rest, darling." Buddy winked as he got up. "Hope we helped and didn't warp you none in the process. And girl, you might want to try the library. Those folks got just about everything you'd ever want to know and stuff you don't. You get your hands on a librarian, and he'll sort you out proper. It's been rare, darlin'."

We shook hands all around. I loved old people.

I'd definitely write Joe in the morning. He'd be so proud of me. It had to be close to two in the morning, and I was just thinking about getting up to go when…

"May I?" A man pulled out the chair that Buddy had just vacated. He was a young man but definitely a man. He was blond and blue-eyed. It wasn't a look I usually dreamed about when I dreamed about that sort of thing, which was, like, all the time, but he was so… "I'd welcome the chance to have a minute with the loveliest girl in the room."

I glanced around to see who he might be referring to. He smiled and sat down. That was it: the smile—*his* smile. You'd do just about anything to see that smile again.

"My name is Cassidy." He extended his hand.

I sure was doing a lot of hand shaking.

"Toni," I croaked, because my mouth had somehow gone bone dry while the rest of me lit up like a Christmas tree.

He motioned for the waitress and ordered another round of dishwater coffee. And then something really surprising happened. Cassidy asked me questions. He wanted to know everything about me. Really. Where did I come from? Why was I out by myself so late? Where did I work? How did I end up in Toronto?

"I want to know it all," he said. "You have this thing about you. Tell me...well, everything you're comfortable telling me."

I was instantly interesting.

So I blathered on about the Purple Onion, the orphanage, the Seven, Betty, Joe, how much one of the gentlemen I had just met had reminded me of Joe. Cassidy made the mistake of encouraging me, which then launched me into how much I missed Betty and all the other girls. I confessed that I hadn't said goodbye or written because I was, first and foremost, a coward. I told him about my search to find my parents, about Mr. Tyson, and about how I was Jewish now—maybe.

I must have been drunk on coffee.

Cassidy interjected here or there to keep me going, or just smiled. He was the best listener in the history of listeners. Aside from Betty.

"It seems to me that you're quite the opposite of a coward. You, Toni, are a beautiful and charming young woman on an epic quest."

Wow, hey, that was great. Quest? Yeah, a quest. I liked that.

He asked me about where I lived. I somehow had the wit to be discreet about Grady, her being so private and all, but I did go on about Big Bob and how our coffee was a million times better than the Embassy's and what a great house band the Ramblers were. Finally, coffee or no coffee, I was getting tired. And even though I didn't want to go, I excused myself.

"Well, I hope you don't mind if I come and try the coffee at the Purple Onion one night."

I inhaled and forgot to exhale. For a second it dawned on me that he was much, much older than I was, maybe even in his late twenties, but I dismissed that thought and went right back to paying attention to how to breathe.

Cassidy stood when I stood and pulled out my chair. When he reached for my hand, he placed a five-dollar bill in it.

Wait! What? What was he...?

"Please promise me that you will take a taxi home. It's much too late for a young lady to be roaming the streets of this city. There are always cabs in front of the Embassy at this time of night. Please, I insist."

I blushed and thought of Ethan following me here, but somehow putting me in a taxi was more thrilling and... grown up. This is what grown-up men did.

"Thank you, Cassidy."

"I'll look forward to the next time, Toni."

The next time?

Sure enough, a cab was right out in front. I told the cabbie the address in my most sophisticated voice. Apparently, my sophisticated voice wasn't loud enough.

I had to repeat it three times. I was in a taxi! What a day, what a night. And Cassidy? Hey, practically the most hand-some man in the whole city thought that I was lovely and charming.

Who was I to say he was wrong?

"Do Wah Diddy Diddy"

(MANFRED MANN)

FINALLY, JOE HAD written! Well, sort of.

Dear Toni all is fine here inkluding with Miss Hazelton and she says the rest of the seven are good to. I told her you got a place to stay and work. We are real proud. You keep looking for your folks and keep your nose cleen. Don't be scared of nothing. You got the stuff girl.

Your friend,

Joe

I had to print all my letters to him. He had more trouble with handwriting. Come to think of it, he struggled with printing as well, but I knew he'd eventually get it by sounding out the words as best he could.

Dear Joe,

I miss you very, very much. Thank you for telling me the news about the Seven. I have heard from Betty, and I am going to write her in Kingston real soon and then I will write to the others one by one, as soon as I get over being such a dope about how I left.

Should I tell him I was Jewish now? That I had pretty much found my father and even had a brother? What should I tell him about Grady?

Mrs. Grady Vespucci is my landlady, and she is wonderful. In a weird way, Grady is like Mrs. Hazelton. She is showing me how to "be" in the city. She looks like a movie star and every-body loves her, including my employer, Big Bob. Well, Big Bob especially, I think. There is a real professor who rooms in the house, and he gives me books to read. He says that he has taken it upon himself to further my education and is convinced that I should attend university! Isn't that unbelievable? They are both really nice but very different from anyone I have ever met. Actually, every single person in Toronto is different from anyone I have ever met.

Should I tell him about Cassidy? I'd had my eyes peeled at the entrance for the past couple of nights. I was crazy disappointed when he didn't show. Maybe it was for the best. A man like Cassidy was likely in the market for a bride.

And as thrilling as I found him, I was pretty sure I wasn't ready for marriage yet.

A kindly gentleman suggested that I might find out some information about my mother from the Yorkville Public Library. I've already been once. The library is a fancy place, and it's run by a very elegant man, Mr. Kenyatta, who is an actual African from Kenya! His voice is like music. Mr. Kenyatta has shown me how to use something called a microfiche, and I am looking through death notices in the newspapers, one by one from 1950 onward, for Halina Royce. It's awful. Sometimes I get a little blue, but then I just listen to your radio and I get myself right again. Sort of like back home, eh?

The letter was getting too long. Joe had a saturation point when it came to words, and I might have just hit it. Besides, I still wanted to run to the library before my shift.

Well, write me soon and tell me the news of the others. I am so happy that Mrs. Hazelton is feeling better. Please send my regards to her. Don't worry, I am doing great.

I miss you very much,

Your Toni

Aside from the Purple Onion and my room at 75 Hazelton, the library was my favorite place. I felt safe there.

When I arrived I marched straight over to Mr. Kenyatta. I knew how to operate the microfiche machine and where it was and everything, I just liked hearing him talk.

"Good afternoon, Miss Toni." Big smile. "May I presume that your exploration continues?"

"Yes, sir, Mr. Kenyatta. I'm ready to resume my inquiries." Mr. Kenyatta was one of the few people who didn't tease me for the way I talked. Not only that, but I pretty much understood everything he said. Maybe it was because we were both immigrants to this strange land.

I sat at that stupid machine for almost two hours.

Nothing.

I dragged my bleary-eyed self over to Mr. Kenyatta. "Nothing."

"It is as I feared, Miss Toni." He nodded gravely. "I too have been trying to assist by reviewing the smaller newspapers. I have not been able to find any relevant obituaries thus far. They are not perfect indicators, however…"

"Like, she could have left Toronto and died somewhere else, right?"

"That is certainly a possibility." He nodded again. "However, it may also indicate that Halina Royce is alive and that the next leg of your research would involve locating her current whereabouts."

Alive?

I had never really considered that. Not in all these years. Why not? I felt like I was under water.

Alive?

"Miss Toni?"

"Yes? Geez, look at the time. I've got to get to work. Thank you so much, Mr. Kenyatta. I'm very grateful for all your help. I'll be back soon."

Alive?

"Do You Want to Know a Secret?"

(THE BEATLES)

IT WAS TIME. I had to ask Grady if she knew anything or had ever heard anything about Halina Royce. Failing a good answer there, I'd have to approach my newfound father. The latter scenario seemed seriously fraught with peril. So Grady it was. I was already working up a sweat. Grady was right about my room turning into an oven in the summer. The same thing had happened in the room Betty and I had shared.

Betty.

If only Betty were here. I could talk this all over with her. Betty was a genius at hosing me down when I got all frothed. I turned up the radio a bit louder. CHUM was playing the Beatles' "Do You Want to Know A Secret?" Pretty perfect. Joe's radio was like that. If you listened, really listened, it popped up the perfect tune for the occasion. When the song ended, I made my way to Grady's parlor. I heard voices when I knocked.

"Come on in and join us, Toni," Grady called out.

The professor and Grady were enjoying some refreshment. Vodka and orange juice, from the looks of it. I was getting pretty good at this. I glanced at my watch: 2:00 PM. It could be worse, but then again, I didn't know when they had started.

"Sorry, I didn't mean to disturb you."

"Sit, sit, my dear." The professor got up, waving his glass. "I was just having one for the road before heading off to the mean streets of academe." He drained his glass. "Slant rhyme. Forgive me; poets are powerless in the face of their questionable gifts." He bowed to Grady, then me, and floated out.

Grady patted the ottoman in front of her chair.

"What's up, buttercup?"

And then it dawned on me. How could I have been so blind? "Is the professor in love with you too?"

Grady almost coughed up her drink.

"The professor? Hardly." She twirled the ice in her glass. "Can't you tell, honey?" When it was clear that I had no idea what she was talking about, she explained, "The professor doesn't swing that way."

What way? What did swinging have to do with anything?

"Because he's a poet?" I asked. "Poets are always falling in love and writing about it too. He's been giving me all sorts of books and he writes…"

"No, Toni." She sighed. "Eddy—Professor Zeigler—is not in love with me because he's lonely for his own kind."

I didn't say anything. I decided that this was going to be my new strategy in the face of my intolerable stupidity. I was getting real sick of not knowing what people were talking about. From now on, I'd keep my mouth shut, and in the ensuing, uncomfortable silence, the deliverer of the unknown word, phrase or concept would feel compelled to explain.

Grady drained her glass in one gulp.

"You don't know what I'm talking about, do you?"

I examined my shoes.

"Okay. Some fellas, and gals too, through no fault of their own—though you'll get a lot of argument on that one—anyways, these fellas, and the professor is one of them, prefer the company of their own sex."

"Like a man's man. I've heard of that." So much for keeping my mouth shut.

"Yeah." She winced. "But not exactly. I mean, they like to have intimate relations with their own kind, see?"

See? See what? Oh my god! Really? Was this a Toronto, big-city sort of thing? How could that possibly work? What would go where? We'd had "health education" this past spring at the orphanage, and I just couldn't picture how...

"Eddy's a good egg, but he's a bit lonely is all. Especially since you gotta keep that kind of thing quiet. Stupid, I know, but that's how it is."

I kept quiet.

"I can tell I've shocked the poop right out of you, but you keep coming at me with this stuff. Now, what did you really come in here to talk to me about? Hold on. I'll be back in two shakes." And off she swayed to the kitchen. I could hear ice cubes hitting the empty glass.

The professor? I still couldn't begin to figure out how all that would work, but I was sad that he was lonely because of it.

"Okay, kid, shoot!" Grady fell into more than sat in her chair.

It took me a minute to regroup. "Well, do you remember somebody called Halina Royce?"

"Hmmm. Yeah, sure, kind of, maybe. What's it to you?"

"Well, you probably didn't notice, but that's the name listed on the hospital-release form as my mother."

Grady didn't say anything, but she took a good long swig.

"Grady?"

"I'm thinking."

"People seem to think she was blond, hardworking, maybe kind of out of it," I said, remembering Big Bob's description. "Maybe worse."

"Don't sweat it, kid. People get stuff wrong." She put her legs up on the ottoman beside me. She was wearing her shiny black high heels again. They matched her black false eyelashes. The woman was no end of glamorous.

"Yeah, she was around. Long time ago. Little thing, not tall like you. Took every job she could, but I got to agree she was kind of zoned at times. Not always. She palled around with Scarlet Sue. They looked out for each other."

Did anyone here just have a normal name? Wait, wait! "Do you mean that my mother is, was, like the professor?"

Grady sighed as she lit one cigarette from the glowing embers of the other. "No, not like that. Sue and her just kept an eye out for each other. They sometimes took turns taking care of the..." She stopped cold and stared at me.

"What? Taking care of what?"

Grady leaned back in the chair. "There was a kid. That's what made it rough for Halina and the jobs, see. Holy Hannah! There was a kid. Kid, are you that kid?"

It felt like my skin was on too tight. I sprang to my feet. "Maybe. I don't know. Probably. I need to find out what happened." I was heading for the door. I wanted to know, but I couldn't bear knowing. "Where can I find Scarlet Sue?"

Grady shook her head. "Last I heard, she got busted again." She caught herself. "Thrown in jail. It happened a lot. Scarlet Sue's a grifter—that's like a con artist—and she got picked up a lot, you know? Brooks might know. He was always good to her when she was down." She downed her drink in one gulp. I lingered by the door.

My father was clearly a man of great compassion.

"So"—I reached for the door handle—"I should talk to Mr. Goldman about Scarlet Sue then?"

She didn't answer.

"Grady, thank you for telling me all this. I really appreciate it." I turned. She was asleep. I crept back and took the empty glass out of her hand and stubbed out the cigarette.

I had no idea how she hadn't burned the place down before I got there. Once again I covered her with the sofa throw, but I did not take off her shoes. I'd learned my lesson. If Grady Vespucci ever went down for good, she'd go with her high heels on.

My head was spinning as I hit the sidewalk. Every time I learned something new, I'd trip into an even twistier tunnel. I didn't belong anywhere, or, to be more honest, I didn't like the looks of where I might belong. Enough. I wanted to go home.

Oh yeah, I didn't have one.

"Hiya, sweet cheeks, ya look a little down in the dumps." A bone-thin man who was almost swallowed up by a wickedly large trench coat stepped over to me. Big Bob had warned about this type of person just last week. They were called "pervs."

"I got just the thing for ya!" And at that he opened up his trench coat as I prepared to scream my head off.

It wasn't necessary. The inside of the skinny fellow's coat was completely covered in jewelry! He had dozens of dangly earrings, necklaces, ladies' watches...wait. What was that? I stepped closer, and the salesman encouraged me to try on anything I liked. "Nothing like something shiny to lift a girl's spirits!"

I picked up a gold chain that had a lovely star hanging from it. "Is that the Star of David?"

"Well, sure, yeah." He was sort of hopping from one foot to the other, causing his stock to jingle and dance.

"It's a star and my name's David. More important, it's 47 karat gold, sweet cheeks. Can't do better than that. You'll be a star when you wear it."

"How much?"

"Five dollars."

"Five dollars!" I was crushed.

"Look, I know you're a lady that knows quality when she sees it. This here is solid gold. It's Italian by way of Egypt and then, uh, Israel, of course. Nothing finer anywheres. Whaddaya got?"

I hadn't been paid for the week yet. But I wanted that chain so bad my teeth ached. It would be a deeply spiritual connection to my new people, plus it was pure gold and pretty. I dumped out all the money in my change purse. "Only a dollar thirty-five."

"Sold! I got me a fatal weakness for lovely ladies. Here, I'll help ya put it on."

I paid the gentleman and walked away taller, straighter and shinier. Things were looking up. My Star of David was my new special thing. And it would stay a secret thing until I had a drawer full of evidence to lay out in front of Mr. Brooks Goldman. And then and only then, I would share it all with him. I'd explain how I knew that he was my father and that I forgave him. And then he would embrace me, and then he would cry, and then I would cry.

And then, best of all, Ethan would feel just awful.

"I Saw Her Standing There"

(THE BEATLES)

IT WAS ANNOYING. I mean, it shouldn't have been. What did I care? Still, it was annoying that I was annoyed.

Ethan was ignoring me again.

He pretended to be busy with the stage and sound equipment. It struck me while he was fiddling with the speakers that he had soothing hair. Like if you touched it, you'd feel better. Ethan's hair was dark, not as dark as mine, but dark, and it was a cross between curly and wavy and shiny under the lights. Not that I thought about it much.

Ethan could afford to stay away now that the infamous Rachel had returned from running away with her trumpet-playing boyfriend. Rachel and I manned the floor while Ethan went back to doing whatever he did before she took off.

I liked her right off, even though she cried a lot and not all that quietly either. Rachel was a hard worker and totally efficient, but she cried nonstop. "Why didn't anyone warn me?"

she'd wail. "The bum!" The patrons didn't seem to mind. Actually, they didn't even seem to notice, which led me to believe that Big Bob was right. They'd been through all of this with Rachel before.

"Don't go near a trumpet player, or any kind of horn for that matter." We were at the espresso machine. "I mean, run, don't walk, as soon as one smiles at you."

I promised that I would indeed run from any fast-approaching, smiling trumpet players. She hugged me. "I like you, Toni." And then she started sobbing again.

I kept trying to catch Mr. Goldman's eye before the first set but couldn't. Finally, the set ended and I started to make my way backstage after him. Out of nowhere, Ethan caught up to me. "Hey, Toni, look…this is stupid. I just want to say…"

Mr. Goldman was heading for the back door. He liked to smoke his hand-rolled cigarettes out there sometimes. I only had a minute. "Uh, sure, Ethan, but I just have to have a word with your father first."

"With my old man? Why? You still on about that?" He threw his hands up. "You're hopeless." He walked away, shaking his head. "The girl's a flake. Deal with it, Ethan."

Was he talking to himself? *Flake*? Like snowflake? That was sweet.

I followed Mr. Goldman outside. Sure enough, he was taking a long drag on his cigarette.

"Toni? Is something the matter?" He sat down on an oil drum.

"Oh no, sir."

He smiled and took another drag. "Good. We all like you, you know. You're doing great here."

"Thank you, sir." I felt an overwhelming sense of family connection with him. Way more than I had with Mr. Tyson, to tell the truth. But now was not the time to get into that. "Grady said that you might be able to help me find someone who knew my mother." Should I tell him my mother's name? Gauge his reaction? No, that would be rushing again.

He took another drag, closed his eyes and nodded. "Sure thing, Toni. Who do you want to know about?"

"I believe her name is Scarlet Sue. I don't have a last name, I'm afraid."

"Old Sue! What a dame!" Now he was smiling with his eyes closed. "Man, the Village was full of great characters back in the day. Better days, better days." Then he opened his eyes and sighed. "Unfortunately, Sue got picked up so many times that the last sentence was for a hard, long one." He took a last drag and then stubbed out the teeny piece that was left. "Worse yet, she was hauled off to the Andrew Mercer Reformatory for Women. A real snake pit of a place." Mr. Goldman shook his head. "There was nothing I could do. She's still there, poor doll."

"Is it in Toronto?"

"Sadly, yeah. Man, they should just blow it up, but yeah, it's here and she's there."

"Oh, that's great! I mean, not that she's there, but that she's there and I can write or maybe even see her."

He stood up. "Stay away from that hole, Toni. Write, if you got to, but that's no place for a girl like you."

"Yes, sir, thank you, sir. Well, I better get back to my tables. That was a great set, Mr. Goldman."

I dashed back inside and searched for Ethan. I caught him by the sound equipment. "Hey, what did you want to talk to me about anyway?"

He didn't even turn around. "Nothing. Forget it."

"Fine." I put my hand on the Star of David under my turtleneck and stormed away in my best huff, which would have been so much more effective had I not tripped over the speaker wires.

He was going to be so, so sorry when I put all the pieces together.

I was still huffing back to my section when I felt a hand on my wrist. "What's a guy got to do to get a cup of coffee in this place?"

Cassidy! Two things flashed at the same time. First, did he see me trip, and second, just as important, was I wearing lipstick? I looked tons older with lipstick.

I had almost given up on him. "Hi, oh hey, hi!" *Really, Toni?*

He looked even better in the Purple Onion than he had in the Bohemian Embassy.

"I've been away on business, but I came in as soon as I could to see you in action."

"Is there a problem here?" It was Rachel. Her mascara was all over her face, but at least she wasn't leaking fresh tears.

"No, no, not at all! Rachel, this is Cassidy, he's a—a friend." Cassidy smiled at Rachel, and I could tell that it was a direct hit. He was, technically, sitting in her section. I looked at her imploringly.

"Nice to meet you, Cassidy. I'm sure Toni will fix you right up."

"I'm sure she will."

He winked at her before she turned, and she winked back at me.

"I make a mean cappuccino. Interested?" *Whoa, I defy Grady to pull off a better line. Everybody look, look! I am handling this so well!* Especially considering that he still had his hand on my arm and Ethan was glaring at me from onstage.

"*You* interest me, Toni." He leaned back in his chair, and I couldn't help but notice how good he looked in the leaning. "How goes your quest? I hope you're getting somewhere."

He remembered! Wow! "Oh, kind of, but not really." Wait, did he say that *I* interested him?

I ignored three of my own tables in the rush to the espresso machine. The Ramblers busted into their cover of "I Saw Her Standing There" and I sang right along with them.

"I smell trouble." Rachel shook her head as she opened Coke bottles. "That man's way too good-looking for his own good. Is he a trumpet player or musician of any kind?"

"No, I promise." I started foaming the milk. "He's a businessman. Isn't he dreamy? I met him at the Bohemian

Embassy. I didn't even know anyone could look like that. It's the smile, don't you think?"

"Yeah, I know what you mean..." But she looked doubtful or sad. I didn't know Rachel well enough to tell which. "I just got a feeling is all, but then, you got to consider the source, and I'm more wrong than I am right, right?"

"Rachel?"

"Yeah, babe?"

"You might want to fix your eyes a tad. They're a bit..."

She started to tear up again.

"What?"

"Nothing. You're so sweet is all."

My hand shook like an earthquake as I handed Cassidy his coffee. He pretended not to notice. "Thank you, Toni. I wish you could join me." He pretty much emptied the sugar canister into the cup. I liked that, since I did it too. "Sadly, I have some commitments, so I won't be able to stay for the whole set."

Was Ethan still watching? I hoped he was.

"But the next night I get free, I would like to take you to the Minc Club after your shift. I think you'd like it a lot."

Was that a date? Was he asking me out? *Seventeen* magazine had all sorts of advice about this. I should play it cool, check my calendar, say I'd have to get back to him, look like I was conflicted.

"Wow, that would be great!"

One of my regulars, who hadn't been served yet, was giving me the stinkeye. "Sorry, I have to go and..."

"Of course." He raised his cup. "Until we meet again." He blew me a kiss right in front of everybody and everything. My heart almost stopped.

Was this what love felt like? Okay, kind of fast, but it went like that in my head all the time. When it's right, it's right. I couldn't get back to the table to clear until almost the end of the set. Cassidy was long gone.

But he had left me a ten-dollar tip!

Ten whole dollars! Oh my god! I could buy a whole new outfit with that! And I would. I had to look my most absolute best from here on in. I would be ready for Cassidy whenever he came in. My whole world was opening up. I couldn't wait to write to Joe and tell him about my progress and how well I was doing and, well, all about this.

Joe would tell everybody, and they'd all be so proud. Actually, they'd be shocked out of their brains. I'd been in Toronto by myself for weeks and weeks, and I hadn't gotten into trouble once!

"It's Over"

(ROY ORBISON)

THE PROFESSOR HAD to knock on my door again in the middle of the night. Given that we had this pact that he would only come up if he were truly alarmed by the screaming, I felt extra humiliated as I peeked out. "It's okay, professor. I'm okay. I am so, so, sorry."

"Not at all. Think nothing of it, my dear. I am truly heartsick that you have to endure this nightmare ritual." The professor was in his pajamas and a very fancy dressing gown with an emerald-green satin collar. Come to think of it, the professor was always a "snazzy" dresser. "Do you remember them when you're awake?"

"No, sir, not really." I rested my head against the door. "There's fire and glass and I'm being hurt on purpose. Nothing makes sense." I didn't tell him that sometimes I could actually feel the glass shards cutting me. Or that I knew it was my mother who was hurting me.

"Well, it's only just past twelve. You can still get a good night's sleep in. Good night."

The door shut and I was in my big, dark, silent room. Alone. The city, unlike the country, did not serenade me with wind whistling through the birch-tree leaves, with crickets arguing or snowy owls surveying their domain. Here in the big city, it was like I was in a vacuum-sealed container. Where was Betty, who grudgingly, sleepily, would always let me crawl in beside her when I got like this? Malou, Sara, Tess, Dot and Cady were not snoring and snuffling in the rooms across the hall. When I was awake in the night and trying to breathe through my fear, I'd heard their heartbeats. And it calmed me. Being together rendered us all invincible. Yet I couldn't wait to leave, to get out *there*, to begin...

Be careful what you wish for. Joe had said that all the time. I never knew what he was talking about then.

I climbed back into bed and turned on the radio real low. It was so hot. The air lay on me like an unwanted blanket. I tossed around, searching in vain for the cool side of the pillow, until I finally went down for the count. I didn't wake up until Roy Orbison mournfully belted out "It's Over" at 9:30 AM.

Not a great way to start the day.

My plan was to spend a few hours at the library, hunting down leads. But by the time I hit the downstairs hall, I heard voices in Grady's parlor. It wasn't even ten. Grady was rarely up before noon, let alone up and entertaining visitors.

I had to knock and find out what was going on.

"Come on in, kid. We were just talking about you."

Whoa!

"Good morning, Toni." It was Big Bob. He'd broken out a new T-shirt again. You could always tell because, even though he liked them tight, you could still see the marks where they had been folded in the package. Far more shocking was Grady.

Even at this hour, Grady looked like she was in the middle of a photo shoot for *Good Housekeeping* magazine, the "How to keep your man happy" edition. She wore a silk organza shirtdress with yellow roses all over it, cinched in with a wide belt made of the same material. Even more startling was that there wasn't a refreshment in sight. Big Bob didn't drink, so there was Grady sipping on a cup of coffee!

"Have a scone, honey. I baked them fresh this morning."

Grady baked?

In the morning?

"Nobody bakes like my Lady Grady." Big Bob got up and helped himself to a couple.

I took a scone and sat down, speechless.

"So how goes the search for your people, kid?" He was addressing me but smiling blindly at Grady.

I filled them in on my new tip about Scarlet Sue and how I was going to get Mr. Kenyatta to help me write to her. This led to a discussion about the evils of the Andrew Mercer Reformatory for Women. We didn't talk about why Scarlet Sue was in there, mind you, just that it was a writhing cesspool not fit for humans.

"How about on your dad's side?" he asked.

I looked at Big Bob, then to Grady and back again. Surely I could trust these people. They had been nothing but good to me.

"Well…" I finished chewing my scone and cleared my throat. "I think I know for absolutely sure who my father is, probably."

"Really? That's great, kid!" Big Bob got up for a third helping.

"Now, Bobby, remember the child was absolutely convinced that Ian Tyson was her daddy."

That got his attention.

"Yeah, well, that was just crazy," I said. "I mean, I love Mr. Tyson, but he's so not my father. That was a ridiculous, childish fantasy and I'm sincerely appalled with myself. Mr. Brooks Goldman is my father."

Nobody said anything.

"I'm absolutely sure of it."

Big Bob dropped his scone. "Brooks?"

"Excuse me." Grady got up. "I need a refreshment."

"Look, Toni, uh…" Big Bob winced. "I don't think that…"

"I have this playbill, and he knew all about Willa's, and he loves music, and I love music, and he has blue eyes, and I have blue eyes, and…"

"When were you born?"

"September 13, 1947, sir."

Big Bob shook his head and was joined in the head shaking by Grady when she came back with her "orange juice."

"No, honey." Grady took a decent gulp. "Brooks was still married to Ethan's mom back then."

"Yes, but I have read that married men sometimes, on occasion—"

"Not Brooks," they both said at once.

Big Bob clasped his hands. "You never saw a man crazier about a woman in your life. If he could have breathed for her, he would have."

"Ain't it the truth." Grady nodded. "She could bore the bark off a tree, may she rest in peace, but Brooks worshipped her."

Big Bob cleared his throat. "You see, that whole year leading up to the time you were born, Brooks never left Elaine's side. Ethan's mom, well, it was a long death, a bad passing. We all looked in for months, sent food. The ladies"—he smiled at Grady—"all took turns with Ethan, who was just a toddler. Day and night, night and day, every day. No, Toni, Brooks would burn in hell before he looked at another lady—no offense."

"But..."

I was about to marshal my arguments, except it was instantly clear that I didn't have any. I didn't even have any proof that they knew each other. My so-called facts went up in smoke. What was the *matter* with me? I'd gone off half-cocked on yet another fantasy. They were both looking at me with real pity.

So, I didn't have a father—again. Wait, did this mean I wasn't Jewish? I had to lug all those books back to the library. I was almost finished *Exodus* by Leon Uris, and I was pretty sure that I was a Zionist.

I liked being Jewish.

Wait, wait. This meant that I didn't have a half brother either.

Ethan.

Well, to be honest, I wasn't sure how I felt about that part.

⁓

I stumbled over to the library in a daze. Truth be told, I was getting pretty sick of the roller coaster I had put myself on. Wasn't I the one who'd always said that I didn't want to find my parents? Did not care, thank you very much. I knew that I had a crazy, violent mom, and my dad was likely just as crazy, for all that I wanted him to be a fabulous musician.

But the thing was, now that I'd started, I couldn't stop. It's like when you lose a tooth and your tongue keeps going to that hole no matter how many times you tell yourself to stop. So there I was, in front of Mr. Kenyatta's broad, beaming smile, explaining how I needed an address for the Andrew Mercer Reformatory so that I could write to one of the inmates.

Mr. Kenyatta did not offer any opinions on the horrors of that institution, and when I told him how the others had described it, he just nodded calmly and said, "I've seen worse, Miss Toni."

We left it at that.

He brightened right up when he asked about the professor, who had, on occasion, frequented the library. "I believe he mentioned that he lives in the same residence as you do yourself, Miss Toni."

"Yes, sir, Mr. Kenyatta. The professor has been very kind to me. He gives me books every week, and I write him little essays about various poems or short stories. He says he's just using me as a guinea pig for his course alterations, but I think he knows he's keeping me from getting too lonely. It's just me and my radio most of the time."

"Yes, he is a fine, fine man." Mr. Kenyatta was scanning his file cards, but he was still smiling.

"Should I tell him you said hi?"

"If you so wish, Miss Toni. Here's the address. Is there another item I can assist you with today?"

He wasn't a big talker, but he had a voice like a cello, which made me unreasonably homesick for the classical music that Mrs. Hazelton always played in her cottage. It was unreasonable because, let's face it, the only time I was ever in there was when I was in trouble. Still, the music was nice.

"Yes, sir, maybe. Have you ever heard of a restaurant called the Noronic?" I leaned on the counter. "A real fancy place. I have the menu. They served things like Dover Sole Almandine and Oysters Rockefeller. Grady says that's all upper-crust type food."

"That is indeed elegant fare, Miss Toni," Mr. Kenyatta agreed. "But I do not recall a dining establishment in this city that is named the Noronic."

"Well, maybe not now. It could be from a long time ago, like the late forties or early fifties."

"Ah! I'm afraid I did not reach these shores until 1958. I will endeavor to locate it or its history for you nonetheless."

"You're the best, Mr. Kenyatta!" We checked out my books and then I thanked him again. I raced back home. I didn't want to be late for my shift, but this was important.

The professor had a glass in his hand as he opened the door. "Ah, books, and not the ones I loaned you. Did you come to see if I was pleased? I am. It warms me to know that you are devouring the great works. I must insist that you consider attending university."

"See, you talk like him too!"

"My dear?"

"I've got to dash, but Mr. Kenyatta—you know, the librarian, who is the nicest man in the world and has a voice like a cello, and maybe he's a little lonely—anyway, he says hi. Seems to me you two would have a lot to talk about. Gotta run."

Okay, so maybe I didn't understand a lot of the things around me. But I understood happy when I saw it.

"Four Strong Winds"

(IAN AND SYLVIA)

I WAS WEARING one of my brand-new Honest Ed's scoop-neck T-shirts (three for $4.99), and Ethan had been looking at me funny ever since I'd come in. I'd bought them the previous day at the store's end-of-July "Super-Duper Summer Steals!!!" sale. The top was tomato red, and Grady approved of it, but now I was worried. Was it too much—too little, too tight, too "hoochie"? The scoop didn't scoop much, but it still scooped.

Ethan came right up to me after the first set. "You've got a blotch on your chest." He pointed to the middle of his own chest. "It's green. Other than that, you look nice."

He hadn't talked to me in days and this was it? I took it as an apology and decided to forgive him his many transgressions.

Rachel nipped over. "He's right. Here." She handed me her makeup compact and beetled back to her table.

I opened Rachel's mirror and gasped. There was, indeed, a green blotch on my chest. "I'm marked!" I fumbled with the chain clasp. "God's punishing me for being a *fake* Jew!" I caught Ethan's eye before he turned to help me with the chain. I'd lingered over the word *fake* hoping that he would grasp the fact that I knew I had made a mistake. Again.

"Nah." At least he smiled as he handed my necklace to me. "God is punishing you for buying fake gold."

Neither the chain nor the star was very shiny anymore.

Ethan, for once, didn't roll his eyes. Instead, he reached under the counter for a tea towel and dotted it with liquid detergent before handing it to me. "Why did you get it?"

"I bought it when I thought I was Jewish and everything." Again I paused, letting the import of the word *thought* sink in. "And it was a star, and I bought it from David."

"You bought something from Dodgy Dave? Oh, honey..." Rachel was back. She was making an espresso, but there were tears in her eyes when she headed back to her customer.

"What, what?" I turned back to Ethan.

"Don't mind her. My dad says that the last ring she got was from Dodgy Dave. It was as fake as the proposal."

"Oh, I feel bad. She was doing better."

"Don't. Rachel's great, but she's a crier. That's just how she is." He shrugged.

He looked all sensitive and sweet and, well, seriously cute, what with all the shrugging and almost smiling. That thought was followed by instant guilt until I reminded myself that we were no longer brother and sister.

"How about I walk you home tonight? Just to keep you safe from Dodgy Dave?"

I felt myself turning the color of my top. "Sure, that'd be nice."

"Great. Then I'll let you in on a secret."

"What? I love a secret!"

"Tyson's dropping in for a short set with my dad."

"Really!"

"Yup, wants to get one in before he and Sylvia head off to New York again."

"Just think of it." I sighed. "Both of my fathers onstage at the same time!" I took off just as he tossed the wet towel at me.

Secret or not, the word must have got out, because the place was packed within minutes. Rachel and I were racing back and forth to the espresso machine all night.

I didn't even see him until he touched my back. Somehow, he had snagged a table to himself. And in my section.

"Cassidy! Hi, hello! Are you here to see Tyson?"

"No, I'm here to see you. You look especially pretty tonight."

My back was warm from his hand.

"I was hoping to show you the Minc Club tonight. Can you join me for an after-hours coffee? I'd like that very much."

Ohmygod. Ohmygod. This was definitely a date! He was here asking and everything!

"I'd love to." I felt thirty.

The rest of the night flew by. Even when my two "dads" got onstage and sang a couple of songs together, it seemed to be over in a minute. Time only stopped when they ended with "Four Strong Winds," with Mr. Goldman singing harmony like the last time. The crowd went berserk again, and I started tearing up. I was turning into Rachel. I didn't know what it was about that song, but it tore me up as soon as the first chords hit the air. I gave my head a shake and cleaned my station and my tables in record time. Thank God Ethan had warned me about my splotch.

Ethan.

Cassidy was waiting by the door for me, but I couldn't see Ethan anywhere.

"Coming?" He extended his hand.

"You bet." One last quick glance around. The guys were milling about the stage. Big Bob was chatting to Mr. Tyson, and Rachel was crying in their general vicinity, but no Ethan.

I did, however, hear a plate clatter to the floor just as Cassidy held the door open for me.

I did not look back.

The Minc Club was way different from the Purple Onion and even the Bohemian Embassy. It was just as smoky but way snazzier. *Snazzy* was my new favorite word. For starters, the furniture matched, and the patrons looked more slick. Everyone seemed to know Cassidy. I felt older, taller, on his arm. We had barely sat down when a waitress appeared. Cassidy ordered a cappuccino for me and an espresso for himself. The waitress was so gorgeous and big in the chest area that I felt myself shrinking into my chair. Plus she was flirting with him. In the middle of all her furious eyelash batting, she asked him if he wanted a little "extra" in his coffee, which seemed to annoy him. She ran right off to get our orders.

I was glad that he was annoyed with her.

People were looking at us. That felt good, except that I had to make sure to hold in my stomach the whole time.

When our coffees arrived, Cassidy raised his cup to me. "So, Toni, what do you think of it? Do you like it?"

"Oh yes, it's very...much more than...quite a bit more..."

"Cool, sophisticated?"

I nodded at him.

"I'm glad you like it. A girl like you deserves only the best."

I was definitely writing Betty first thing in the morning. I'd apologize my brains out and then tell her all about this!

"How old are you, Toni?"

Uh-oh. Was he worried about our potential—okay, very real—age gap?

"Sixteen. But I'll be seventeen real soon." Cassidy raised an eyebrow. "No, really—in September. How old are you?"

"Older." He smiled.

There was music playing in the background, even though there was no one onstage. They must have had a very expensive sound system and someone working it. It was jazz, good jazz. Joe would love it here. I would bring him here the minute he got to Toronto.

Cassidy was asking me about my progress on my quest when an unusual-looking gentleman walked up behind him and placed his hand on Cassidy's shoulder.

"My boy."

Cassidy made to get up, but the man kept his hand on his shoulder. "Sit. Relax. Who is your gorgeous companion?"

It was completely understandable that the man got that part wrong, because even though he was wearing the most beautiful suit I'd ever seen on anybody, he also wore black sunglasses. I mean, the club was already darker and smokier than the Onion was, and he was wearing sunglasses! And then, when it hit me, I was flooded with shame.

"Toni, this is Mr. Marcetti from Detroit. He owns a piece of this place."

Mr. Marcetti smiled and extended his hand in the right direction and everything. "An insignificant portion, dear child. I am a good friend, a benefactor, if you will, of Cassidy's."

"I'm very pleased to meet you, sir."

"I think I may have mentioned that Toni is on a quest to track down her parents," Cassidy said.

Cassidy had talked about me? To his *benefactor*? What was a benefactor? That was like family, right?

"Ah yes, the orphan girl. I am very sorry for your troubles, young lady." He smiled right at me. "Please order anything you like, on or off the menu. My treat. And I would be so pleased if you could both attend one of my parties."

A party? A real party?

Cassidy looked away.

"All the best people come. Who is your favorite musician?"

"Mr. Tyson, sir, Mr. Ian Tyson."

"Oh, Ian frequently drops by."

"Toni works at the Purple Onion, Mr. Marcetti."

"Ah. And when are your nights off, if I may ask?"

"Sunday and Monday nights, and Wednesday is a half shift, sir." Was that too much information? "Are they very fancy parties? I don't have very fancy clothes…"

Cassidy just put his hand on mine, and I shut up.

"Not to worry." Mr. Marcetti bowed his head slightly. "It's been a rare pleasure. Cassidy, I'll leave it with you then." Mr. Marcetti left us but continued to stop at tables for a word here, a word there. He didn't bump into a single thing. The man was a miracle. And he had very nice manners too.

"Wow. Isn't he just…wow?" We were on our second round of coffees.

Cassidy kept smiling at me. I seemed to amuse him—a lot. That was a good thing, or at least it must have been, because he would also reach for my hand every so often. I worried that he could hear my thumping heart every time he touched me. It made me crazy nervous. "I have never seen a blind man move so well. 'Course, I only knew the one, Emmet, back in Hope? Well, he had the glasses and the dog and the cane, but poor old Emmet wasn't anywhere near as steady on his feet as your Mr. Marcetti."

"What?" Cassidy stroked the top of my hand with his thumb, but he looked kind of distracted as he did it. "Toni…"

"Yes, Cassidy?"

He didn't say anything for a bit, and I didn't feel I should say anything again for fear of breaking the mood or the moment or whatever we were having.

"It's late. Time for a young lady to go home." Again, he slipped a five-dollar bill into my hand. "I'm afraid I have to stay."

"But I can walk. I know my way around the—"

"It's too late." He shook his head. "Please, I need to know you're safe." And then we both got up and he was going to kiss me, yes he was. A girl, even an orphan girl who pretends she doesn't have any fantasies, well, except for that one, can tell these things. He wanted to kiss me, and I *wanted* him to kiss me. It would be my first kiss. I'd been waiting practically my whole life for my first kiss. I needed to be kissed. I held my breath and closed my eyes and…he did not kiss me. Instead, he brushed a stray strand of hair out of my eyes. "Take a taxi."

I could have sworn he was going to kiss me.

"I Want to Hold Your Hand"

(THE BEATLES)

I WAS PERSPIRING so much that my bare feet left footprints on the floor. I was also pacing, which didn't help the sweating thing. Betty had written me weeks ago. It had been forwarded from Loretta's Diner, which had been set up as our postal drop. Joe had let them know my address as soon as he got my first note. I'd torn up five previous attempts. But this time I was going to do it. I was going to write her back. Hence the pacing.

I sat down and devoted the first page to apologizing and asking for forgiveness for A) sneaking away without saying goodbye and B) not writing back sooner. Then I paced some more.

Now my hands were wet.

Things are so unbelievable here in Toronto that I don't know where to begin! It's all good, mainly. Well, actually, it's a bit of a roller coaster, and I'm still having the nightmares.

*But still good, you know? All in all, I'm pretty proud of myself.
Like, there's a billion people in this city and I even know some of
them! I have this amazing huge room, but I'm the only one in it,
which is good except when I'm lonely and when I have the dreams.*

*Anyway, when the dreams are bad (you know, me screaming
my head off), a very nice man who is a professor of literature at
the University of Toronto comes down and knocks on my door
until I wake up and answer it. Isn't that sweet? I live in sort of
a rooming house, but it's just me and the professor who board
here. Mrs. Grady Vespucci owns 75 Hazelton and she is the most
beautiful woman you could possibly imagine, except she drinks
a bit too much. She calls them "refreshments" but they're spirits,
Betty, no two ways about it. Grady gives me fashion advice
and life advice and I tell her most everything when she hasn't
over-refreshed.*

I wrote her about Big Bob, Mr. Kenyatta, Crying Rachel
and even Ethan, but I felt myself heating up even more, so
only a word.

*Ethan is the son of Mr. Brooks Goldman, who is this
amazing musician whose band, the Ramblers, plays at the
Purple Onion all the time and who, embarrassingly, I thought
was my father for a minute. I also thought that Ian Tyson
was my father (same amount of time). Don't ask—it was
HUMILIATING! I know, I know…I'm the one that teased
you all for your stupid orphan fantasies, but get me out of
the orphanage and I become a champion fantasizer! Maybe*

it's the alone thing. So in the end, unlike you, I haven't made much progress in finding out who my real father is or was, and I haven't tried real hard on the mother front. Actually, I am trying to track a lady down who was her best friend, but it's complicated—she's in a ladies' prison!

I am so glad to hear that you are well settled with people who care about you. I am even gladder to hear that you have a young man! David sounds wonderful and the FIRST KISS sounds spectacular (I'm so, so jealous)!!! I have a young man, too, except he's older, maybe quite a bit older! Cassidy (it has just hit me that I don't know what his last name is!) is a businessman, and he might be almost thirty! I know, I know…But he is SUCH a gentleman, and everybody looks when I'm with him because he is so handsome, and I'm not exaggerating for once. He is going to take me to a very posh party one day, and I'm already fretting about what to wear. He hasn't kissed me yet—as I say, he is a true gentleman. He is very, very interested in my story about being an orphan. He really cares. I believe he will try to help me.

I had to get up and walk around again. Did I sound all braggy about Cassidy? The truth was that he was thrilling and exciting and…he scared me a little. But I liked that too. I hadn't talked about him to Grady, which felt kind of like a lie. Mrs. Hazelton always said that a lie of omission was just as bad as a flat-out whopper. I'd been "omissioning" a lot, and while it didn't used to bother me much with Mrs. Hazelton, I felt guilty about it with Grady.

Anyway, anyway, I miss you to pieces and more. Actually, I miss all of us as an "us" more than I ever thought possible. I dreamed of being away and on my own, of having my own room, for such a long time and now that I finally have it…well, it's just not like I thought it would be is all. Tell your fella I said hi and to treat you like a queen. Good luck at your end with everything, and write me soon if not sooner.

Love you lots,

Toni

xoxox

Okay, so see? This was why I didn't want to write. It all sounded stupid on paper. If only I could see her, talk to her. Here it was, almost August, and I was no closer to finding out anything about who I was or where I came from. All this time I'd thought that I didn't want to know anything about my father or about her. Now, writing about my lack of progress, I truly realized that I did.

I mean, who was I?

Why was I?

A girl's got to know these things.

I folded the letter and shoved it into an envelope and addressed it to Betty's new home.

Home. With a family, a *real* family, to belong to.

I showered and got myself done up in my second new scoop-neck T-shirt, the royal-blue one. Grady approved of it the most. I slunk out of 75 Hazelton. I could hear the professor and Grady speaking softly. They were busy. They didn't need me always barging in on them.

Come to think of it, no one needed me.

Snap out of it! I hated it when people got all droopy drawers, but I especially hated it when I did. So I gave my head a shake, plastered on a big smile and marched to work. Still smiling, I combed the place for Ethan. Even when he was mad at me, Ethan made me feel "real." Besides, I felt awful for taking off on him. As usual, he was fiddling with equipment onstage.

"Hey!"

Nothing.

"Hey, I looked all over for you last night, but I couldn't find you. Look, I'm sorry about…"

Ethan stood up. He was holding a couple of screwdrivers. "Who's the old guy?"

"The old…oh, that's Cassidy. He's a friend."

Ethan nodded. He didn't get all snotty and holier than thou. He looked right at me for a bit and then shook his head. "Okay." He nodded. "I got it." And he walked away.

Wait. What?

"What? Ethan, wait!" But he kept on walking.

The place was filling up fast. I had to start on my tables. "Ethan!" But he did not turn around. And I couldn't figure out why it mattered so much. But it did.

"Universal Soldier"

(BUFFY SAINTE-MARIE)

TWO DAYS LATER I was back at the library. Mr. Kenyatta was looking especially fine, sporting a navy-blue suit and red paisley tie. "Hi, Mr. Kenyatta. You look really nice today."

"Thank you, Miss Toni. I will be taking my Canadian citizenship test later this afternoon, and I feel that one should look as dignified as the occasion demands."

"Which reminds me, I said hi to the professor for you and he says hi back. Well, he actually said to send you his *kindest regards*, which I figure is even better, right?" Mr. Kenyatta busied himself with a file folder, but if he could have blushed, I think he would have.

"I have significant news for you, Miss Toni. I have managed to unearth the mystery of the *Noronic*." He slid the file folder over to me, but he looked pained as he did so. It was bursting with marked newspaper clippings. I went to flip it open, but he put his hand over the folder.

"Might I suggest that you go to one of the tables to peruse the clippings in private?"

"Why, what is it?"

"We could not find the *Noronic* as a fine-dining establishment because it never was one, Miss Toni. The *Noronic* was a vessel that sailed to various ports of call on the Great Lakes. It was considered the most beautiful passenger ship in all of Canada."

"But that's great! It all makes sense. The dinner menu would be from the *Noronic*'s dining room. You're absolutely amazing, Mr. Kenyatta. What a breakthrough!"

But Mr. Kenyatta did not look amazed with himself.

"Was, Miss Toni. It *was* the most beautiful passenger ship in the country." He finally met my eyes. "On September 14, 1949, when the *Noronic* docked in Toronto, hailing from Detroit, it caught fire. The vessel and the city were ill prepared. It remains, to this day, the greatest single tragedy in Toronto's history. Over 150 souls lost their lives in the fire."

Fire? A fire? Mr. Kenyatta continued to speak, but it was just like my last meeting with Mrs. Hazelton. I heard the music of his beautiful voice, but I couldn't make out the actual words. Was that it? Were my parents on board? They had to have been, or why would I have the menu? Was that the fire of my nightmares? The shattering glass?

The words stopped after a time, and Mr. Kenyatta led me to a table with a reading lamp at the far corner of the library.

I wanted to throw up on it.

When I got a better grip on myself, I opened the folder. The clippings were yellowed and curling, orphaned from their newsprint homes. Each was tagged with the date and source. But the photographs...the photographs were depictions of hell. I picked up a clipping from the *Toronto Daily Star*, dated September 17, 1949.

160 DIE IN SHIP FIRE IN TORONTO HARBOR

Fear Bay Hides Bodies of Many Who Leaped Heroism and Horror Mingled as Flames Sweep S.S. Noronic Firemen Comb Ruins for Dead

Nearly 200 persons perished in the fire which destroyed the S.S. Noronic, biggest pleasure ship on the Great Lakes, at the Canada Steamship Lines dock in Toronto early today. This was the estimate of firemen as they cut their way through the charred and twisted wreckage.

Fire Chief Peter Herd said there was "no telling" how high the death toll will go, and it might be two or three days before the fate of all the 550 passengers and 180 crew members is known.

~~Bodies were being taken off the blackened~~ ship by the score...

I had to put the clipping down. Were my parents' bodies among all those corpses? Those poor, poor people.

SHATTERED GLASS

Went Up Like Paint Factory

"It went up like a paint factory," said one witness. British United Press quoted survivors as saying fire extinguishers failed to work when they grabbed them from the walls to battle the flames sweeping through the hallway. "There was negligence on somebody's part," the news service quoted Don Church, Silverlake, Ontario, as saying. Another passenger said the extinguisher he seized had no fluid in it...

My mind swept to the panic and horror of the passengers on board. What a contrast to the fire at our orphanage. How orderly we were in comparison, a bunch of kids and a couple of adults. The Little Ones all did as they were told, just like we had practiced. And we Seven...me, Malou, Sara, Dot, Tess, Cady and dear Betty, my sisters...No one could have asked for more from us.

Burned beyond recognition.

Tarpaulins were used to carry the dead off the deck after they were carried there by firemen. Some were burned beyond recognition. In some cases only bones were found.

Police officers and firemen, who lifted the remains into the improvised stretchers, which took two and three bodies at a time, were visibly shaken. "I hope I never see that again," said one officer, his face white...

Apparently, many of the dead remained unidentified. Even if I found and combed the death lists, I couldn't be completely sure one way or the other. I closed the folder. I wanted to *unsee* what I had just seen; failing that, I wanted to run. But there was no riverbank for me to run to. I had to sit with the images, with the horror. Is that where my nightmares were born? On the *Noronic*? I didn't know how long I was rooted there, wincing at flames that no one else could see.

"Miss Toni?" A gentle hand on my shoulder. Mr. Kenyatta's hand. "It's late. I have the citizenship exam to attend, and I believe you have your work."

I got up slowly, happy to have Mr. Kenyatta lead me out of the stacks. We went our separate ways when we hit the street. I hope I wished him good luck. I hope my manners kicked in automatically. I don't remember.

It was busier than usual at work, and there was no time to talk to anyone. A singer named Buffy Sainte-Marie was coming in for the evening set with the Ramblers. There was a lot of excitement around her tune "Universal Soldier," a haunting and powerful song that she actually wrote in the Purple Onion. People started piling in really early in order to secure a table. Rachel was scurrying from table to table and only crying intermittently. Big Bob was meeting and greeting like his life depended on it. Mr. Goldman was understandably preoccupied with the evening's sets and his guest artist. And Ethan still acted as if I had a contagious disease.

I needed Betty. I needed the others. They would make sense of the *Noronic* and what it meant or, at the very least, just hold me.

I needed a hug.

I did my work, made and hauled espressos and cappuccinos, cleaned tables, joked with customers, all with flames still licking the corners of my mind. I barely noticed how magnificent Buffy Sainte-Marie was onstage. Nobody once asked how I was or anything about me. Why would they? I was nobody to them. Why would anyone care?

Would there ever be anyone who cared?

The fist gripping my heart loosened as soon as I saw him. Cassidy. It was near closing. He was standing at the back wall, arms crossed, with a smile that was meant only for me. "Hey, you look like you need a friend and a jolt of happy. Come to the Minc with me."

I didn't hesitate. "You bet!" I cashed out in record time. When we got outside on the muffled, silent streets, Cassidy didn't ask what was up or quiz me. He just put his arm around me. "It's okay. Whatever it is, it's okay. You're with me now."

"She Loves You"

(THE BEATLES)

EVERY SINGLE SLINKY lady in the club, plus all the waitresses, kept "accidently" bumping against the back of Cassidy's chair on the way to the washroom or wherever. It's a burden being with a fella who's prettier than you are. Cassidy seemed oblivious to all of them. I tried my best to be polite and ask him questions about himself, but he kept waving me off. "You seem upset, Toni. What's happened?" He kept asking and encouraging me until I told him all about the *Noronic*.

Cassidy reached over and put his hand on mine as he listened. I loved it when he did that. It felt tingly but safe, comforting and thrilling, all at the same time. It also had the bonus effect of stopping all the accidental bumping into his chair.

"Tell me about your people here, Toni. Surely you have people keeping an eye on you, watching out for you?"

"Oh no, not at all! I mean, they're great, and they've helped me out, but they're not kin or like the Seven. I only got to Toronto in June, after all." But that didn't feel quite right either. So I launched into a peppy description of my generous landlady, the patient professor and the resourceful Mr. Kenyatta. I got up a real head of steam on the swell people in my life.

"And you think Big Bob is all tough as nails, but he's been such a pussycat, and Mr. Goldman has been unbelievably sweet, and he got me onto the Scarlet Sue thing. But they're not family, and it's not like at the orphanage," I repeated. "They can't be expected to keep tabs on me. I never in a million years thought I'd miss that."

Cassidy raised an eyebrow. "And how about Goldman's kid?"

"Ethan?" When was the last time we'd talked or he was even near me? It struck me that I missed him being near, the feeling I got…"We're barely friends."

Cassidy squeezed my hand. "I'm glad."

My heart stopped at the hand squeeze and needed a moment to start up again. "So yeah, I'm alone and all, but I've met many fine-quality people straight off the bus." I didn't want him to feel sorry for me, after all. "Toronto is a wonderful city, full of helpful and truly kind people." Okay, I'd gone from being down in the dumps to doing a happy dance in three sentences. Even I was having trouble keeping up with myself.

Thank God I was interrupted when the nice blind man, Mr. Marcetti, appeared at our table. Cassidy jumped to his feet. "Mr. Marcetti, please join us." He pulled out a chair, which was really thoughtful given Mr. Marcetti's condition.

"Just for a moment." He looked right at me. "Ah, the beautiful Toni." The man was amazing. "What have the two of you been discussing so intently?"

Cassidy looked away. He seemed to be concentrating on the empty stage. "Well, sir, we were just reviewing Toni's current situation and her lack of connections in the city. Sadly"—and here Cassidy actually did look sad—"sadly, our Toni has made no progress in hunting down any links to her father or mother."

Our Toni?

Cassidy began fiddling with the little plastic spoon that came with his espresso.

"Ah. I'm genuinely sorry to hear that, but perhaps this will cheer you up," Mr. Marcetti said. "I believe I mentioned my parties to you the last time we met?"

I nodded eagerly, until I remembered that the poor man was blind. "Oh yes, sir. You did, sir."

"Well, some of my guests would certainly be of your parents' vintage, and they are powerful people who knew the lay of the land in the old days." He smiled in Cassidy's direction. "Perhaps one of my guests would be able to help with your search. I'm having a special party next Sunday night."

Snap! The little spoon that Cassidy was holding broke in two. He turned to Mr. Marcetti. "I'm not sure that Toni is in the right frame of mind for a—"

"I'd love to go! Can we go, Cassidy? Please? Maybe someone will know something."

Mr. Marcetti turned to Cassidy. "It seems your young friend would be delighted to attend."

"Then I would be delighted to escort her, sir."

Why weren't we all happy here?

"Excellent. I look forward to seeing the both of you." Mr. Marcetti got out of his chair and flawlessly made his way to another table. He joined a group of men who were all smoking and discussing something with a fair amount of intensity. Each wore sunglasses. Was it a special outing of some kind?

"I know I've said it before, but Mr. Marcetti is absolutely—"

"Toni, he's not blind."

"He's not?"

Cassidy sank deeper into his chair and shook his head.

"And those other gentlemen with the black sunglasses are not...?"

More head shaking.

"But why would they wear...?"

"It's a look some men, some businessmen...it's time to go."

He was angry.

I didn't blame him. It would be embarrassing to be at a swell, sophisticated club like this with a girl who was too stupid to breathe. I went rigid trying to remember all the dumb things I must have said to Mr. Marcetti.

"You don't want to take me to the party. Are you annoyed with me?" I asked as he pulled out my chair. "I wouldn't blame you. I annoy a lot of people."

"Annoyed with you?" He looked puzzled. "No, Toni, I'm not annoyed with you, not at all."

He took my arm as we headed down the stairs, and my heart soared. "Can we still go to the party?"

He turned to me in the gloom of the stairwell. "Sure, Toni. Yeah, we'll go to the party."

I wanted to jump up and kiss him, but since he hadn't kissed me yet, that would have been unseemly and patently overeager, even for me. What would Sara advise? She was the only one of us who'd had a real live boyfriend. I settled for trying to sigh prettily. "I don't see any taxis."

"Well then." He smiled. "I'm going to have to walk you home tonight."

There was still something wrong, but as long as it wasn't me, I didn't much care. A car rolled by with a Beatles song blaring out of its radio. "*She loves you, yeah, yeah, yeah…*" It was almost embarrassing. I tried to look away, but Cassidy winked and put his arm around me again. I would definitely have to tell Grady all about him. At some point.

The streets were deserted. I had a thousand questions about the party, but I used all my willpower to keep my mouth shut. He, too, was quiet, lost in thought. It was like we had the city all to ourselves. Every so often Cassidy would stroke or squeeze my arm, but every so often he would also shake his head and sigh. Just a little. I didn't think he even knew he was doing it.

Steam rose up off the sidewalks and disappeared above the fogged streetlamps. It had rained while we were in the club, but it was still hot. We walked through the smell of warm, wet tar, accompanied by the fading sounds of cars whooshing through puddles on faraway streets. I vowed to remember every single detail. They would be the sounds and scents that I would always associate with this night, this city and the sad, handsome man who had his arm around me.

"Navy Blue"

(DIANE RENAY)

IT TOOK ME a while to track down Dodgy Dave. Rachel and Big Bob had been egging me on—insisting, actually. I found him on Wellesley Street, just outside of Queen's Park, showing his wares to people who looked like they actually worked in that pink castle building.

"Hey, Dave!"

"Hey, Star of David chick!"

Wow, not only did he have an excellent memory, but he didn't seem the least bit embarrassed or caught out. That gave me pause, but I'd been practicing, so I didn't let it stop me from chewing him out in front of potential customers for selling me jewelry that had turned my neck green. Even then Dodgy Dave didn't lose his cool.

"Okay, chickie, you got me. What can I do to make up for it?"

Well, that had gone better than expected. Big Bob had coached me on various scenarios, and here Dave had just up and folded in front of me.

"Oh. Uh, I need a pin for a gentleman who has just become a Canadian citizen. He passed his exams and everything."

"Lucky for you, my little bunny"—Dave reached into an inside pocket in the great big trench coat—"I got this little baby. It's an artist's rendering of the top three designs for the new Canadian flag. Perfect, huh? It'll be a keepsake to be passed down from generation to generation."

It was beautiful. Mr. Kenyatta would love it. "I'll take it! How much?"

"Come on, kid, you were doing fine right up until then." We had attracted a few extra bystanders. "You done real good reaming me out and now you blow it by asking me how much. Start again."

I cleared my throat. "It'll do." I shrugged uncertainly. "So, uh, I'm going to take this pin as compensation for the, uh, other item that was a grievous mistake on your part."

He groaned, but he gave me the pin. "Look, kid, you got to get yourself some grit, or you won't survive out here."

Was a con artist giving me advice?

Besides, I'd always thought of myself as being chock-full of grit. "Yes, sir. Thank you very much."

He groaned again. "Take it from me, not everything or everyone is what it appears to be."

I nodded politely.

"Especially if it's pretty and shiny. You paying attention?"

"Yes, sir. Can I really have the pin?"

Sigh. "Yeah, go, get lost. You're bad for business."

"Thank you so much!" I headed straight for the Yorkville Public Library. What a city! Even the con artists were sweet.

"Miss Toni!" Mr. Kenyatta beamed at me as soon as I burst through the doors.

We walked back to the reference desk together. "You did it, didn't you, Mr. Kenyatta? You're a Canadian citizen."

He beamed again.

"I have a little present for you." I pulled the pin out of its miniature plastic bag. "It's like the three official renderings of our new flag. As you know, we don't officially pick one until the end of the year, but it'll be from one of these three. Isn't it great?"

"It is indeed." He pinned it to his lapel. "I will wear it with pride every single day, Miss Toni. I am beholden to you. That was most considerate."

"No, not really." I shook my head. "It's not one of my shinier qualities. But I try real hard to make up for it."

"I have a little something for you too." Mr. Kenyatta slid a piece of folded paper over to me. "The lady you were searching for in the Andrew Mercer, your Scarlet Sue?"

"You found her?"

"Yes." He nodded. "Scarlet Sue's real name is Miss Susan O'Reilly. She has been incarcerated in that unfortunate place for almost nine years. I believe I have procured the correct telephone number for you to call and request a time for visitation. As I understand it, if Miss O'Reilly is not in solitary confinement—what the prisoners call the dungeon—she will be allowed to see you if she so wishes."

I thanked him and slipped the paper into my purse, surprised by the sense of urgency I felt.

"A word of caution, Miss Toni. Miss O'Reilly has apparently spent a great deal of time in the dungeon, for various infractions. The gentleman I spoke to took a fair measure of delight in telling me she got what she deserved for not *playing along proper like.*" Mr. Kenyatta paused. "He was an odious gentleman, and I fear it is an odious place. Do prepare yourself."

Was I really going to go to a prison?

"Thank you again, Mr. Kenyatta. I'm always thanking you."

"And it is always my pleasure, Miss Toni. But please consider this step carefully."

"Yes, sir, I promise, really."

I couldn't get home fast enough. I was sure that Grady would let me use her telephone.

"Grady?" I knocked on the parlor door. "Grady, it's me. Can I please use your phone? Grady, are you there?"

"Keep your toga on." She opened the door and then swept back into the room. Grady was wearing one of her more glamorous ensembles. A stiff navy-blue silk dress that flared out dramatically at her tiny waist and, of course, her shiny black high heels. Her makeup was flawless, and her blond hair spritzed and teased within an inch of its life.

And she was clearly refreshed. Weeks and weeks of watching Mrs. Grady Vespucci up close had let me in on the telltale clues. Grady was swaying on the inside.

This was what she described as "the sweet spot." Thing was, she rarely stopped there.

"How about I make us a coffee and tell you about my visit to the library."

"Coffee?" She looked crestfallen until I told her that we had tracked down Scarlet Sue and that I was going to visit her and finally get some answers.

"You're going to the Mercer?" She sat hard on the kitchen chair while I prepared the coffee.

"Yes, ma'am. If she'll see me. Scarlet Sue is the best I've got in terms of leads. Don't worry, everybody's been warning me about the place, and Mr. Kenyatta even said she might not be right in the head on account of spending a lot of time in solitary. They call it the dungeon."

Grady shivered.

I placed her cup beside her on the kitchen table. "Grady?"

"At the Kingston Pen, it's called 'administrative segregation.' That's where my first husband was. The guys call it 'the hole.' He was put in there a lot in the early days. A lot." I could tell she was eyeing the bottle of vodka on the counter behind me. "It changed him. He was…unrecognizable after a time."

Did I dare?

"Grady? Is he—is that maybe why you drink so much?"

"Is that why I drink? Ha!" She rose quickly and headed for the bottle. She opened it and poured a splash into her coffee. "Is that why I drink?" She was angry now. "Hell,

I wasn't the one in the hole. And I got remarried and then remarried and remarried! I got this beautiful place and all the money I'll ever need, right?" She waved her arm around the kitchen. I remembered what Big Bob had told me about her subsequent husbands. The last two were "meaner than snakes."

"Honey, I drink 'cause I'm a flat-out coward."

What? No. Grady was spectacular, and she was strong. Any fool could see that. What did Dodgy Dave say about pretty shiny things? Well, he was dead wrong, at least when it came to my landlady.

I took her by the arm and led her back to the chair. "I don't believe it, not for a minute, Grady. You're beautiful and kind and gentle and...really beautiful. Everybody thinks you're like a queen or something!" Her eyes watered, but no tears broke through. Grady wasn't a crier, not even in her various states of refreshment. She shook her head and gulped her fortified coffee.

"Yeah, yeah, yeah." She waved me away. "Go make your phone call, kid. Go on. You can never brace yourself for whatever's coming. And sometimes it's just best not to know."

"A Hard Day's Night"

(THE BEATLES)

IT WAS THE hottest day in August, and that was saying something. But not here. The waiting hall of the Andrew Mercer Reformatory for Women was cool, but not the kind of cool that was a relief from the furnace outside. The prison was the clammy cold of weeping stones and sweaty crumbling mortar. I sat waiting on a long low wooden bench with what looked to be a family—a father and three daughters. We were all shivering. This was an evil place.

Why had I come?

A guard marched in with a clipboard. "Visitor Antoinette Royce for inmate Susan O'Reilly." It wasn't until the family all turned to me that I realized he meant me. The name, my full and formal name, still fit like those too-big shoes I had worn when I walked away from the orphanage. Someone else's shoes.

I followed him through a long narrow passageway. I was scared, no use pretending otherwise. I was scared of this creepy place and scared of what would meet me at the other end of the passageway. Grady was shaken by the memory of what "the hole" had done to her husband. What kind of half-human would greet me?

I was led to a small near-empty room. A table with a wooden chair on either side beckoned. The guard grunted in the vicinity of the chair and then stepped back and knocked loudly on the door opposite me.

I wanted to run. Instead, I held my breath.

The door flung open and a redheaded apparition strode in, grinning from ear to ear, arms outstretched. "Lord Almighty, give me strength! Antoinette Royce! Give your auntie Scarlet a hug, honey!"

"Oh, I…"

The guard took a menacing step toward her. "Sit down, ladies. Now!"

Scarlet Sue shrugged and plopped into the chair. "Give your butt a rest, girl. They don't mess around in here."

Did I sit? I must have, but it would've been with my mouth open. Despite wearing a bleak gray uniform, in this even bleaker room my impression of her was one of riotous color. Of course, there was her hair, which was indeed scarlet and seemed to have a life of its own, shooting out of her head in tightly sprung coils. But it was more than that. It was like she had swallowed a rainbow.

"Hally's baby girl! Lord oh Lord oh Lord. I haven't seen you since you were a roly-poly toddler." She couldn't stop grinning. The smile revealed teeth that were crooked and one tooth that was broken, but that didn't diminish its power a bit. "I just wish that we coulda met under better circumstances. And I regret that now, baby girl. I really do." She shook her head. "I was only supposed to be in for four to five. If I'd only known…if I'd known that there'd be a chance, I'da smartened up for sure!"

She knew me. This was someone who knew me—or had known me. "So what happened?" I hadn't even said hello or asked how she was or said it was nice to meet her. Mrs. Hazelton would've keeled over from shame.

She *knew* me.

Scarlet Sue did not seem to take offense at my lack of manners. "Hell's bells, I escaped a couple times, don't ya know. They don't take kindly to that here, do they, Sam?"

The expressionless guard almost smiled.

"Stop shivering, girl. I'm scaring the pants off ya, ain't I? Or is it Sam? He has that effect." She placed her arms on the table and exhaled. "Look, I'm happy to just sit here and look at you, but since you tracked me down, I assume you want to talk turkey, and they don't give us long. Do you got a list of questions or something? I'll tell you anything I can."

A list. Yes. That would have been smart. "No, ma'am, but I've got…" I reached into my purse, and the grim guard was at the table in an instant.

"You can't be reaching into your purse like that, honey," Sue said.

"But they already checked it all out before I got to the waiting hall."

"Just tell smiling Sam what you want and he'll have to get it for you."

What was I doing here? "Just the three pieces of paper, please." He reached in with his gigantic paws, placed the papers on the table and then stepped back to the wall.

Scarlet Sue examined the birth certificate, the *Noronic* menu and the Willa's poster at great length. I felt vaguely ashamed, although I wasn't sure why.

She raised her eyes from the papers to me. Hazel eyes, etched by lines and fissures but pretty eyes nonetheless. "Antoinette. Is that what they call you?"

"No, it's Toni, ma'am."

"Ha! That's what I called you!" She sat back and rocked a bit. "I wiped your runny nose and taught you how to curse like a sailor." She chuckled at some far-off memory while I wondered whether that little fact explained my so-called attitude problems at the orphanage. "So, Toni, what do you know so far?"

"Almost nothing. Until a couple of weeks ago, I thought the *Noronic* was a restaurant."

Scarlet Sue stopped rocking, and all her color seemed to drain onto the stone floor. "Right. The *Noronic*. Okay. So your mom and dad were married in Detroit. They were Americans, which I guess makes you one too, come to think of it. Your dad came from money, big money. 'Course, your mama did not, but God she was a looker and the sweetest spirit on earth. Didn't matter though. The Royces forbade the marriage, so your mom and dad eloped. Needless to say, the family cut them off. Your dad's people had him real late in life and they were kind of controlling, to put it mildly. Cut-off-their-noses-to-spite-their-faces types."

"Five minutes, ladies."

No. There was so much…

Sue flashed Sam a look. "Your father *was* training to be a lawyer, join the old man's firm, but he was a gifted musician, see? Apparently, he really had it going on with the tenor sax. Your mama encouraged his dreams even after they had you. Anyways, they drifted from club to club, barely scratching out a living in and around Detroit, and then he got a real good gig offer in Toronto at that place, Willa's, long term, leading the house band." Sue tapped the torn poster. "It was their big break, and the icing on the cake was that Jordon—that was your father, Jordon Royce—got hired to play on the *Noronic* on the way over from Detroit to Toronto."

At the mention of the *Noronic*, our guard moved closer to us.

"So my father would have been like Mr. Goldman after all." I said it more to myself than to her. "The Ramblers are the house band at the coffeehouse I work at."

"Brooks? Hey, give him a shout for me, eh? Yeah, sure, your dad, he woulda, coulda…Well, you know about the fire, the disaster?"

I nodded.

"Yeah, so, the fire was this nightmare inferno, as Sam here could tell you. He was there." Sam was at our table now.

If there were an extra chair, I think he would've pulled it up and sat down. "But what came after…that's what broke her, you know?"

"Three minutes, Sue."

She shot him another look.

"Look, rules is rules. I'm sorry."

"You almost drowned in the rescuing. For all I know, it was Sam that fished you out of the drink. He was part of the rescue team. Your mom made it out, half out of her head until she found you, but your dad…" She sank farther into her chair. "They couldn't find him, see? Identifying the bloated and burned bodies was a…problem." She looked uneasy. "Look, Toni, I don't think I—"

"I'm not a baby anymore! I need to know!" I said that with a bit more force than I had intended. "Please, I want you to tell me."

Sue groaned at the ceiling. "So, for days and days, your mom searched for him, body by body. They set up this disgusting staging area at the exhibition grounds. It was an unholy mess. Rows and rows of charred and water-swollen bodies. Hardened war vets and cops wept like babies. Apparently, the stench and fumes rising off of the dead was worse than at any slaughterhouse."

"Rotting, fried, wet flesh." Sam was shaking his head like he was there, seeing it all over again.

"Day after day, she looked for him in those putrid, pus-filled halls, with you in tow. The doctors, what did they know then? They were likely trying to help, but they gave her all sorts of pills. Miltowns, Valiums. How could she get through it otherwise?"

It felt like she was telling me a story. That was it. It was just a story. One that had almost nothing to do with me. I was far, far removed from it. Oh, I nodded sympathetically at both the guard and at Sue. It was a sad story, unbelievably tragic, but all it was, was a story until...

"Time's up."

Sue ignored him. "She found him on the eighth day. The only way she could identify your father was by this cheap wedding band she'd bought for him. They cut off his finger so it could be identified by his initials."

Oh God.

Sam tapped the table. "Sorry."

"They had to pull her off the, uh, remains, and you were just toddling around from one, uh, person to another. Hally was never the same after that."

Was that my nightmare? Was that the fire, the shattered glass? Could I have a memory from when I was so small?

"Time's up." The guard went to the back of my chair.

"No, wait, please. What about after, the couple of years after...?"

"Look, they'll have my ass in a sling," Sam growled. "You gotta go."

What about when she tried to kill me?

"I'll write you, Toni. I ain't much with a pen, but I'll write. Where are you at?"

"I'm renting a room at 75 Hazelton, care of—"

"At Lady Grady's? Tell her I say hello. She's a good broad. I'll write ya. Stay there." Sam had her by the arm. "Stay there, okay?"

Where else would I go?

Sam knocked loudly on the far door, which opened immediately and swallowed up Scarlet Sue. Then he led me out through the corridors, the waiting hall, the front hall and outside. Free.

I was seared by the sun. Stunned, stupid and blind. My father…

"Toni? Toni, you okay?"

He never got to play at Willa's. Never even set foot… My father was dead. He'd been dead all along.

"Toni!"

It was Ethan. He stepped over to me, close. "Having a hard day's night?" He smelled of sun.

"What are you doing here, Ethan?"

He shoved his hands in his pockets and spat. He spat just like Joe. "Don't get your knickers in a knot. I didn't want to be."

"Oh."

"Grady called Big Bob, and Bob got all up on my old man that you were coming down to this place and…" He shrugged.

And they made him come.

"And oh yeah, your old guy came looking for you when we opened. Rachel told him you took the day off." He spat again. "So, you ready?"

I was simmering with a rage I could taste. No, it was the taste of soot. It filled my mouth, leaving no room for words to explain my anger and confusion. He *was* a musician. What my young father, full of hope, had gone through, what my mother…but no, that was the confusing part. I couldn't, didn't, want to feel sorry for her. But…

I wanted to hurt someone.

I took a faltering step, smacked Ethan's chest and started to sob. What was he going to do? The poor guy had no choice but to put his arms around me.

"Louie Louie"

(THE KINGSMEN)

IT WAS EMBARRASSING for both of us. I mean, extremely. I went straight into an ugly, snot-streaming cry, and neither of us had a handkerchief or a tissue. I just slobbered on his shoulder, babbling incoherently about the *Noronic* and my dad and bloated bodies. When I had nothing left but hiccups, I stepped back and tried to apologize.

"Your shirt's a mess." Sniffle, sniffle. "Sorry."

Ethan shrugged. "Don't worry about it. That bad, eh?"

I shrugged back at him.

"Home?"

"Sure." We walked to the streetcar stop in silence, rode it in silence and then walked all the way to 75 Hazelton in silence. I was grateful to him for that. I tried to tell him that he didn't have to walk me home—it was daylight, after all, and he was already late.

"Nah, it's okay."

It was pity. I was an exceptionally superior judge of pitying facial expressions, and I could tell that Ethan was wearing one.

I hated pity. We, all of the Seven, hated pity. Never pity an orphan.

"So, uh, thanks," I said when we got to Grady's. "See you tomorrow, I guess."

Yup, I was pretty sure it was pity.

I was dragging myself up the stairs to spend the rest of the night in my room and have a proper, *private* pity party when Grady stepped out into the hall.

"Toni? Would you like to join me for dinner?"

I came down a couple of steps. Was she feeling sorry for me too? I wanted to feel sorry for myself all by myself.

"It won't be a regular occurrence, so don't get all excited or count on it, you know. It's just that I baked a whole chicken and it looks like Eddy went straight to the bars after his classes, and I know you usually grab something at the club so…How about it, just you and me, kid? You don't have to talk about…well, you know. I mean, you'll have to tell me at some point, but not now."

"That'd be real nice, thank you." I followed her through the parlor door and into the kitchen. Grady was a little less done up than usual. She wore a peach-colored sheath; it looked like she had raided Jackie Kennedy's closet.

"Not here, dear. We're going to eat in the dining room. Go sit; it's all ready."

"Yes, ma'am." I'd never been in the dining room before, just glimpsed it through the glass-panel doors. There was a massive mahogany breakfront that held the fine china and elaborate figurines. The table, which could seat at least twelve, was covered with an ornately embroidered tablecloth. There were two settings, one at the head of the table, nearest the kitchen, and a setting to its immediate right. It was set formally, with wineglasses, water goblets and an array of forks, spoons and knives, linen napkins, a crystal water jug and silver salt and pepper shakers. We'd been taught at the orphanage how to set table for all manner of occasions. Miss Webster had drilled it into us hard. I guess the thinking was that we'd likely end up becoming maids, waitresses or well-trained housewives. Grady kept swanning in with trays—chicken, potatoes, vegetables and a salad.

"Sit, dear, sit. I've just got one more thing."

"You've set a beautiful table, Grady," I called out after her.

She waltzed back in with a large glass of wine in one hand, and her cigarettes, lighter and an ashtray in the other. "That's thanks to my third husband. He'd beat the crap out of me if I had the fish fork out of place." She took a sip of her wine and grimaced as she sat down.

"I've never seen you drink wine before." I poured water for both of us.

She took another sip and shuddered. "I don't. Can't stand the stuff, but I'm turning over a new leaf, and wine's supposed to be good for you. The French drink it nonstop. It doesn't even count as booze." She glared at the glass.

"Did you buy a bad bottle?"

"Shouldn't be." She took another sip and shrugged. "It was the most expensive bottle they had, but what do I know? Want some?"

"No, thank you, ma'am, I don't drink."

"'Course ya don't. Well, let's not stand on ceremony. Dig in!"

It was delicious. She had stuffed the chicken with lemons, of all things. Grady really and truly could cook. She and Joe would have a lot to talk about. And so did we. In between mouthfuls of food, I told her that Scarlet Sue said hi and then, before I knew it, I told her everything. She only got up once to replenish her glass, at which she was grimacing less with every sip. I told her about my mom and me and the fire and my dad and searching for him and... finding him.

"Doesn't get much grimmer." She shook her head. "So what now, kid?" she asked at the end.

"I don't know, Grady. I honestly don't. Scarlet Sue said she'd write. They only gave us a few minutes to talk. I don't know what happened after my dad died. Thing is, I don't know that I want to know."

"But you've come so far. I'll grant you it's a heart-hurting story. But it's *your* story. You gotta find and face it head-on, or...or you'll end up making a mess of things."

Was she talking about me or her?

She didn't know how badly the story ended. How could she? "No, you don't understand. Look." I pulled the scoop neck of my T-shirt down far enough that the scars would be visible.

"Oh honey, what the…?"

"I've always had 'em. They're nothing now compared to how they used to be when I was little."

Grady quietly took another sip.

"I get these nightmares," I continued, "but I don't know if they're nightmares or if I'm actually remembering stuff. A fire, glass shattering and my mom, my *mother*, hurting me bad."

"Eddy mentioned the nightmares. I am so sorry, but you still—"

"See, I've hated her all my life for doing this to me and then deserting me, but I guess I maybe understand how she could have turned crazy or whatever. Truth is, Grady, I don't know how much more of my story I can stomach."

Grady put down her glass, got up and hugged me. "You can take a lot. You got to, and so do I."

"Excuse me?"

"I'll be right back. I need a proper refreshment for this." Grady returned with her more familiar highball glass in hand and kicked off her high-heeled sandals. "Remember how I told you how the hole changed my first husband, pretty much left him in shreds? He even divorced me!"

I nodded. I knew that part already from Big Bob. Where was she going with this?

"Well, that's on me, kid. It's all on me." Before I could open my mouth to challenge her, she put up her hand. "See, Mario did kill a guy his papa wanted hit, and there were probably others, but it was me who got him put away. Nobody knows to this day except me, Bobby and now you. I tipped off the cops on the sly, just enough to lead them to the truth, just enough to nail him."

"Grady, I don't—"

"Shut up and let me tell it."

I shut up.

"We were the big love match, right? Ask anyone. We all ran together as kids, Mario, Bobby and me. But Mario was faster and smoother with his moves, so like a turnip I fell for him, and we got hitched. I honest to God didn't know how deep he was into...well, his father's business." She took a swig and then leaned back and looked at the chandelier, as if for guidance. "I'm not saying that there wasn't love, and lots of it, but the boy had a temper. As it turns out, most of 'em had tempers." She snorted. "I'm not saying I didn't deserve it. I was mouthy, but you know, at the end of the day, I didn't deserve it. No woman does. And Bobby, well, Big Bob was always there for me, and that made things worse with Mario. The cops were sniffing around about the Carmine hit, and I got wind that Mario was going to go after Bobby next. Mario was crazy jealous. His best friend...my Bobby." She hugged herself. "I couldn't let that happen."

I didn't know what to say, so I just nodded.

"I did it," she said. "I put my own husband away. So that's my story, kid. Time I faced up to it." She downed her glass. "And you know what? I'd do it again." She seemed to be talking to herself more than me. "Yup, that's the sticky truth of it."

I wished more than anything else in the world that I was older and could say smart, solid words that would comfort her. But I wasn't, so I didn't.

"I'm sorry, Grady."

"Yeah, well..." She examined her glass. "My point is, you make choices...just own up to them. Even when it seems that life is making all the decisions for you, you're still making choices, kid. But, for all that"— she sighed— "the fifties were my era, my time. You should have seen me then, Toni. I was something back then." She drained her glass.

How could she not see herself? "No, Grady! You're *something* now! You're gorgeous and good through and through. You didn't have to open the door to me way back in June. A girl right off the bus from nowhere. You're the only one who did, Grady!" My voice trembled. "The only one! Where would I be without you?"

She waved her hand dismissively.

"If you could only see yourself through my eyes or Big Bob's eyes or, well, just about anyone in Yorkville, you'd never have a single doubt about being *something* again."

"Yeah?" She turned her head away, but I caught a raised eyebrow before she did so.

"Yeah!"

"Okay, okay. Look, all I'm saying is, don't wait until you're forty to face up to *your* story. Now go away."

"Yes, ma'am." I started clearing the plates. It seemed to me that life was definitely making all the choices when it came to me, and lousy ones at that. I washed everything in short order and did a quick cleanup of the kitchen. Grady did not move or speak. When I got back to her, I suggested that she'd be more comfortable in her armchair in the living room.

"You still here, kid?"

"Yes, ma'am. Let's go to your chair."

I got her settled, got her cigarettes and then covered up her stocking feet.

"You're a good kid, Toni."

"Yes, ma'am."

She grabbed my arm just as I was turning to go.

"I mean it, Toni. Find out the rest of your story. You're strong enough for whatever it is. Find it and face it. You're young. Don't hide; don't dodge. It catches up. The shadows cripple you."

I didn't know what she was talking about. "Yes, ma'am."

"Promise!"

I nodded as I reached for the door.

"And Toni?"

"Yes, ma'am?"

"Quit *ma'aming* me, damn it!"

"Oh, Pretty Woman"

(ROY ORBISON)

THE NEXT DAY I found out that I was a high-school graduate. Almost. All I was missing was one course. I got the letter from Miss Webster. Mrs. Hazelton had somehow arranged for all of us to get full credit for the whole year even though we hadn't quite completed it. It must've pained Miss Webster something fierce. She was a real stickler for detail. I had mostly taken courses a year ahead of where I should have been right from the start, so I was only one geography class short of completing all of my requirements for grade twelve.

And I didn't much care.

Betty would have earned all of her credits to graduate. And Betty would care.

Dear Betty,

God, I miss you! Well, first off, congratulations! I know that you got your diploma from Miss Webster already. I am so pleased for all that is going so well in your quest. I mean, you seem to have got yourself a wonderful fella and the family of the house really care about you and...

I ripped up the letter. It was going to be a long list of things going really good for her versus my mess of a story. So...

Dear Betty,

Hey, congratulations on getting your diploma. All is good here. I'm still trying to piece my...

No. No, I wasn't. I wasn't trying to piece together anything, let alone the rest of my story. A letter from Scarlet Sue had arrived along with Miss Webster's, and I hadn't even looked at it. I didn't want to know. I was back to my original nightmare about my mother trying to hurt me, but now I just felt sad for her. Anger was better.

So what I do know is that my father and mother were married. So much for your theory about me being the love child of a famous movie star! Funny thing, though—my father was a musician after all. The story is kind of gut-wrenching...

Actually, the story left me with nothing.

I was adrift without any hatred to hang on to. My hatred of my mother had carried me a long way, even though I had never dared to say it out loud, even though I could barely whisper it to myself.

Was she alive somewhere?

Where?

Did I want to know?

Maybe. I was no longer an orphan, no longer part of the Seven, no longer a daughter who hated her mother. The few shreds of who I'd thought I was were gone. I just couldn't whip up any righteous rage now that I knew what my mother had gone through. I bet I was a difficult child.

I bet I'd want to kill me too.

I ended up writing Betty about everything. I wrote about Scarlet Sue and the Reformatory and everything I knew about the tragedy of the *Noronic*. Even in the writing, it was still like it was someone else's story. As if I was reporting something that may as well have happened to Tess or Malou.

What was the matter with me?

I finished my letter to Betty as best I could and signed and sealed it without reading it over. If I reread it, I'd toss it for sure. I picked up one of the professor's poetry books, opened it and then shut it. I got up, started pacing, sat down and glared at Scarlet Sue's envelope. I got up again. And there it was again—the no-guts thing. Oh, I'd done stuff at the orphanage that *looked* fearless, but it was just stupid stuff. Like getting everyone to sneak out of their rooms and meet up for a cigarette in the garden shed when I didn't even smoke, or recklessly grabbing one of the Little Ones who had climbed on top of the roof. None of that was real. It was pretend.

Joe always said that fake courage was better than no courage. Just remembering him made me look harder for my grit. My shift didn't start for almost four hours. Plenty of time. I needed a new dress, a special dress, for the party at Mr. Marcetti's. Grady said that the only place to go for something that posh was Simpson's. She also insisted that I get myself some cream-colored stockings, because all the young girls were wearing them.

That was it. Shopping! I would find the perfect dress, and I would impress Mr. Marcetti and his guests so much with my fine dress and fine manners that Cassidy would feel absolutely compelled to kiss me—a lot—and then I would know for sure that he was my own true love, and then I'd write Betty nothing but good news for once, and then it wouldn't matter about my story, because he, Cassidy, would love me for whoever I was at the moment and…did I mention that he would kiss me?

I was firing on all cylinders.

I grabbed my purse and Betty's letter, raced down the stairs, ran to the subway and went straight into the most elegant, breathtaking store in the world.

Simpson's!

Every single saleslady had mauve hair, and they all had eyeglasses on long sparkling crystal chains that rested on their bosoms. The glittering, glistening main floor of Simpson's housed the perfume and makeup department. It was a temple of beauty. You could actually spritz yourself for free with the bottles of perfume that sat on silver trays on the counters. I must have spritzed myself with a hundred different perfumes and colognes. I'd never worn perfume before, and I was instantly enthralled by the scents, the packaging and the beautiful names. Miss Dior, Chanel No. 5, L'Air du Temps, White Shoulders, Shalimar...they all seemed to promise something—a story, a much, much better story.

"Put the bottle down, dear." One of the purple-haired ladies touched my arm.

Was I in trouble? Were they were going to throw me out before I even got near the dress department? "I'm so sorry, ma'am." I felt like I'd been caught stealing. "I thought we could try the perfumes. I saw some of the other ladies spritz…"

She made a clucking sound. "No, dear, it's okay. I'm just trying to save you from yourself. You're going to leave here smelling like a parade of working girls."

"Yes, ma'am." What was wrong with that? I worked, after all.

And then she got that look on her face that I could now read at twenty paces. She knew that I didn't know what she was talking about.

"Follow me." She went behind another perfume counter and reached deep into a drawer. "This is a sample of L'Air du Temps. Trust me, it's going to read the best on you. I'm only supposed to hand them out with a purchase, so don't be flashing it around." She handed me an exquisite, perfect, miniature replica of the bottle that was on the counter.

"I'm sorry, but I don't think that I can afford—"

"It's a sample, dear."

It was the most beautiful thing I had ever seen in my life. It had gorgeous little crystal birds stuck to the top of it. I sighed and put it back on the counter.

"It's free."

"Free? Oh! Thank you so much, ma'am. That's incredibly generous of you and this very fine establishment. Grady said that Simpson's was the best there is, and she knows everything!"

I could tell she was trying not to smile. "Are you just looking around or…?"

"Oh no, ma'am. I have money. I'm here to buy a special dress for a party, and stockings too. The stockings have to be cream or white, but I have no idea about the dress."

"Young ladies usually come in here with their mothers for that kind of purchase."

I felt my shoulders slump.

"Or their aunts?"

More slumping.

"Older sisters?"

Would she want the perfume back?

"Never mind. You get yourself to the third floor, the Young Miss Department, and ask for Miss Zelda. No one else will do, got it? You tell Miss Zelda that Mrs. Howland said that you have to be done up proper. Understand?"

"Oh yes, ma'am!"

"And dear…" She opened my hand and dropped another perfect little bottle in it. "Your first perfume marks a very special day in a girl's life. I'm honored that I could be the one to share it with you."

I reached out and gave her a hug, startling the both of us. It felt so good. God, I missed hugs. We Seven were always hugging each other, and we'd hugged the Little Ones nonstop. Yet it never seemed to be enough. I ran off to find the escalator.

Miss Zelda was a wonder. We tried on eleven different "frocks." I loved each one of them, but there seemed to be no pleasing her. She finally settled with some satisfaction on a sleeveless, pale-blue "water silk" dress with an empire waist. "You could easily be a house model, dear. You get tired of the Purple Onion, you just come marching back here, and I'll set you up."

I, of course, had no idea what a house model was, but it reminded me that I had not adhered to Grady's constant admonishments to keep my guard up with strangers.

In the course of our time together, Miss Zelda pretty much learned everything there was to know about me. I also knew that she had a daughter who, now that she was married and lived in a place called Oakville, thought that she was too good for a mother who "schlepped shmatas." Needless to say, she was touched when I told her all about how I thought I was Jewish for a minute, had bought a fake Star of David, read *Exodus* and still wanted to go to a Jewish church one day.

"Synagogue," she corrected. "But you're more Jewish than my Sophie. She's a knife in the heart, that one."

Miss Zelda put my stockings, a slip, the perfumes and my dress into a very fancy garment bag, shaking her head the whole time. She also gave me 12 percent off everything because she said that it was all going on sale in two weeks. And she hugged me too. "Whoever he is, he's a lucky guy!"

Strangers were wonderful people! Grady was dead wrong on this one. I floated out of Simpson's, clutching my purchases and bolstered by hugs.

All the way to the subway, I daydreamed in minute detail about how irresistible I'd look in my new outfit, all freshly perfumed, lipstick on and hair just so. I imagined a thousand different scenarios where my "lucky guy" boldly took me in his arms and kissed me at great length and with great passion. He would put his head here and I'd tilt my head there...or no, farther back, maybe, or to the side a little? Where would our arms go? Should my right hand reach for his neck or rest on his shoulder? What do you do with your left hand? Should I lick my lips first, or was that gross? Were we standing, sitting, leaning?

There sure were a lot of serious mechanics to consider in one's first kiss.

"You Don't Own Me"

(LESLEY GORE)

I DIDN'T HAVE enough time to get to 75 Hazelton before my shift, so I lugged all my goodies to the club. Instead of setting up our tables, Rachel oohed and aahed over my purchases. She had never seen anything as pretty as the L'Air du Temps bottle either, so I gave her one. When I dug out the dress and held it against me, she started to cry.

"You'll look real nice, Toni," Ethan said. Where had he come from?

"She's going to a real swell party on Sunday night." Rachel sniffled.

"Oh," he said. And with that *oh* we were back to the Cold War. "Big Bob wants to see you in his office, Toni."

Uh-oh. I didn't have a single pleasant memory of being asked into anyone's office. I was never one of the girls that Mrs. Hazelton or Miss Webster had asked in for a pleasant heart-to-heart over a cup of tea. And, let's face it, I was still recovering from my last visit to Mrs. Hazelton's office.

I combed my transgression memory box and came up empty. What had I done? My panic was in full bloom by the time I got to the office.

Big Bob's door was open, and he was on the phone. As soon as he saw me, he waved me in. "Here she is now... yeah, you too. Behave yourself and get out of there, hear." He handed me the telephone and mouthed, "It's Scarlet Sue. You only got a minute."

Oh my god, the letter. I hadn't read her letter.

"Miss O'Reilly? Hello? It's Toni here."

"Hiya, toots. Look, I've been tying myself in knots ever since I sent the letter. You got it, right?"

"Yes, ma'am." Well, I had.

"So, I been thinking about it, and I apologize. It probably came out too stone-hard. I ain't good with words on paper."

"Ma'am?"

"The facts about the fire. I only got it all second and thirdhand, you know? I looked for youse everywhere, really I did, kid, but the cops nailed me practically the minute I got over the border, see? It was a short one that time, but by the time I got released, the trail was colder than a brass toilet seat."

Fire? "The fire on the *Noronic*?"

"What? No, the one in your the basement flat!"

"Excuse me?" Dear God in heaven, how many fires were there?

Big Bob hurriedly brought around a chair and then excused himself.

It was a good thing I was sitting.

"The basement fire where you and Hally had been living."

I started to get up and then wisely sat back down.

There was a long exhalation at the other end of the phone.

"You didn't read the letter, did ya?"

I sighed into the phone. "I'm sorry, ma'am. No, I didn't. I wasn't sure I wanted to know. See, I'm not very…I'm sorry."

"Oh, take off your hair shirt, sweetie. You've got a lot to chew on. It's right smart to dole things out in little pieces, so you don't end up choking on it going down."

I nodded at the phone.

"Toni, you there? Smiling Sam here is breathing down my neck even though I ain't ever blown my nickel on anyone before."

I didn't know what she was talking about. I was getting well and truly tired of not knowing what people were talking about.

"Toni!"

"I'm here, Miss O'Reilly, sorry."

"Quit apologizing, and that's a life tip, toots. I'm the one who feels like a dog. Hally was my best friend. Do you want to know now, or do you want to read the letter?"

Did I? Was my mother alive? Did I?

"Yes, I want to know. I mean, please tell me."

"Go to hell, Sam, the kid wants to know."

"Are you okay, ma'am?"

"Yeah, he's gone back to pacing and growling. So, here's the goods as far as I got 'em. Okay, so I was away when it happened, in Buffalo on, uh, business."

"Do you mean when the fire happened?"

"Yeah. You girls had moved while I was gone. Finding rent was always a problem."

"And me? Was I a problem?"

"Sure. Oh, not like you was a brat or anything. It's just that landlords weren't keen on taking on single ladies with a little kid." Then I heard her grumble, "I'd kill for a smoke, Sam. I'll make it up to you later." There was mumbling, then the sound of a cigarette being lit and inhaled. "So, the way I heard it, when I couldn't find youse anywhere, was that there was a fire in one of the basement flats over there in the village, maybe yours, maybe not. And then, honey, the trail went dead. There was a ton of fires in those days, and I mean a ton, see?"

"Uh, no."

"The places were run-down, and sometimes they blew because of bad wiring and sometimes the owners helped it along because of the insurance money. I'm not the only con in the city, kid, but I wouldn't touch that kind of scam. Too dirty."

Huh? There was a piece of me that still believed I had a monster for a mother. There might have been things that drove her to it, I knew that now, but I had a mother who had harmed her own child. "Did she set the fire? My mother, I mean."

"Halina? What? No! I mean, what do I know, but no! Why would she do something like that? She got down a bit at times, and those pills didn't help, but she wasn't nuts and she wouldn't do it for some money scheme. I ought to know. I tried to bring her in on the side with my little cons, and she wouldn't go near 'em."

There was a muffled "You don't own me, Sam, so give me a another minute, will ya?" and then she said, "She'd never risk anything happening to you, kid. You were the only reason she was living."

But that memory, that nightmare. I knew I had that right. I knew it was my mother. I could recall the smell of my own fear. I wasn't wrong about that. Scarlet Sue had been away, after all. Things change; people change.

"When was this—the fire?"

"Well, I left right before Christmas '49, and I got back sometime in the spring."

I stood up again and stayed standing. "I have a hospital-release thingy that says I got out in April. So it's got to be a fire that happened between the beginning of January and the end of April."

"Yeah, it's not much. Like I said, there were a lot of fires back then. It may not even have made the papers. Sorry, it's all I got."

"No, no, that's good, Miss O'Reilly."

"Auntie Sue."

"Yes, thank you, Auntie Sue. I have a genius librarian friend, and I'm sure he'll help."

"Good. And…kid?"

"Yes, uh, Auntie Sue?"

"I don't want to see you down here anymore. This is no place for a girl like you."

"But I'd…"

"Even Sam is nodding his head. You got a question, write me. I don't want to see your face here. In fact, I'll refuse to see you, got it?"

"But you're all I've got, and now that I've found—"

"I mean it! You don't know what you don't know, and you're not gonna learn it visiting me. Not if I can help it. You got it or not?"

Big Bob had returned. He was leaning against the doorway and pretending to survey the back of the stage.

"Yes. I mean, no. I promise I won't try to visit you again."

"Okay then." Her voice was softer, more resigned now. "I'm due to get out before the end of the year, and if I behave myself I may actually do it this time. And kid, I will do it this time because of you. Stay at the Lady Grady's and keep out of trouble." Then there was muttering and cursing. "Right. Smiling Sam has put his foot down. Gotta go."

"Thank you so much for making the effort and tracking me down. It means so much, I can't tell you how much…"

But the line was dead.

Big Bob walked in and put the telephone back on its receiver. "She's a pistol, that one. I'd pay attention to whatever she has to say."

"Another fire!" I stood there. "There was another fire with my mom and me in a basement flat. I'm supposed to find out about *another* fire! I mean, come on!" I wanted to kick something, throw something. "No way." I shook my head. "I'm done. No more."

"Suspicion"

(TERRY STAFFORD)

HANDS. MY HANDS? *No. But someone's hands grab me hard, grip tight, hurt me. Lift me. I struggle. I scream. The hands shove me into piercing glass shards, over and over. "Stay still!" I can't breathe. Little and big pieces stick into me. Others cut me again and again and…smoke chokes me, smothers me. "No, Mommy, no!"*

I was screaming in time with the pounding on the door. I'd done it again, woken the poor man up.

"Coming! I'm okay, professor. I'll just get a robe." My nightie was plastered against me with sweat.

"You needn't open the door, my dear, so long as you're okay."

I still opened it a crack. "I'm okay, thank you. I actually woke myself up. I feel awful. You know how sorry I—"

"Don't apologize, please." He started to walk away and then turned back. "Toni, I fear it's getting worse. You simply must endeavor to find out what happened to you."

I nodded in the dark.

"Toni?"

"Yes, sir. I have been, really, but I know there's more."
I shivered despite the heat, and I told him about my conversation with Scarlet Sue.

"Good. Tomorrow then, first thing."

"Yes. Wait. What?"

"You and I are going back to the library in the morning.
We'll help narrow down the search with your talented
Mr. Kenyatta."

"No…I…the thing is, I'm not sure that…"

"Meet me downstairs at 10:00 AM. Good night."

"Good night." But it wasn't. I couldn't get back to sleep.
Yes, I was afraid of the dreams, but I was way more afraid
of the truth.

⸎

The next morning, the professor, Grady and I sat sipping
our coffee as if we were attending a funeral visitation.
Grady was silent because she wasn't accustomed to being
alive and alert before noon. The professor was reviewing
class notes, and I was mute with exhaustion.

I made a last-ditch stab at convincing them that this
was not necessary. "I actually don't…I mean, I even told
Big Bob that I'm not ready to…"

"Forget it, Toni." Grady had roused herself. "Like it or
not, you've got us involved in this. And kid…" She pulled

her robe tighter around her. "You're just a kid. We may not be your regular-type adults, but we're *your* adults, and we think you've got to get to the bottom of this. I can't have you scaring off the tenants." She drained her coffee. "Toni?"

"Yes, ma'am. Thank you."

She rolled her eyes. "Okay, you two, get out of here. I'm going back to bed."

The funny thing was that even though they knew each other, at least to say hello, both Mr. Kenyatta and the professor acted all super formal when I reintroduced them. "Mr. Kenyatta, I believe you know the professor?"

Mr. Kenyatta extended his hand. "Edward, it is a pleasure to see you again."

"Indeed, the pleasure is all mine, Baraka. Toni tells me that congratulations are in order, that Canada has wisely welcomed you as a citizen."

Baraka?

"That's very kind indeed…"

I slipped away to where the library held its stash of teen magazines. With any luck they'd go on like that for hours and never get to the research matter at hand. I was deep into the big fall issue of *Seventeen* magazine—I had to get myself some penny loafers—when the professor reappeared.

"All done."

"How? I mean, I haven't done anything, looked up anything."

"I gave Baraka the parameters and the few details we have. I also explained that we had a rather reluctant researcher in you. He'll wade through the clippings about fires in the area for all of 1950 and 1951."

"Oh."

He looked at his watch. "As it turns out, I uh, have an early luncheon meeting with someone." He looked pleased and uncomfortable as he glanced over to the front desk.

"I see." I smiled at him. "I really like Mr. Kenyatta."

The professor looked away. "There's a lot you don't know about the world out there, Toni."

"Yes, sir. That singular fact is brought home to me a thousand times a day. I had no idea how much I didn't know at the orphanage. I used to think I was so smart." We started for the doors. "And then I got here and found out that I don't even know how much I don't know."

At least he smiled. He was a nice man, but not big on smiling.

"The thing is, and maybe I got it from Joe or something, I know, when I really, really listen to my gut, I know how to recognize a really good person. And, well, you're one and so is Mr. Kenyatta."

"And your gut tells you this, does it?" He looked amused. "Perhaps you know more than we give you credit for."

With that he went on his way. I'd lied, of course. Oh, not about him and Mr. Kenyatta, but about listening to my gut.

Truth was, I'd been doing my level best not to listen to it. Truth was, I'd been passing off my gut's early-warning system as gas.

I decided to hustle over to the Purple Onion and start my shift early. The espresso station could use a thorough cleaning. Cleaning would get my mind off things. By the time Rachel and Ethan came in, you could have performed surgery on any surface in the place.

Neither of them noticed.

Rachel was rattling on about a new fella and how this one might be the *one*, for absolute sure. "And he's not a musician, Toni! He's got a real professional job."

"That's great, Rachel. What does he do?"

"He's a vacuum-cleaner salesman! Well, that and water-filtration systems and a bit of real estate on the side. A real professional type."

"That's terrific. I mean it. Well, I'm going to tidy up the supply closet now. There's still time before we open."

The supply closet was always cool and dry, and I was exhausted from worry and lack of sleep. I wanted to lie down on the floor. Instead, I lost track of time sorting out napkins, sugars, salt and cutlery.

"Hey, we've opened."

Ethan leaned against the doorjamb. He wasn't looking at me, but I was looking at him. He'd filled out a bit over the past couple of months. He was going to be very handsome one day.

Like today.

"Wait, before you go…" He straightened up and made actual eye contact. "I just wanted to say…to apologize or call a truce or…"

"Are we at war, Ethan?"

He shrugged. "I'd like to try to be friends." He shrugged again.

"Try?"

"Yeah, try. I'll try, okay?"

He looked rather stricken for someone who wanted to be friends.

"I'd like that, Ethan. Truce it is."

"Good, good." He smiled. Ethan had dimples that appeared when he smiled a certain way. I wanted to touch them. Then the smile evaporated, and he dug his hands into his pockets. "The old…uh, your boyfriend is out there looking for you." He walked away.

Wait. But…

Cassidy, no doubt about it, was a real handsome man, a real man period. He didn't have dimples, but when he smiled like he did as soon as he saw me, he sucked up all the light in the place and then beamed it back out.

"Hey, gorgeous." He was playing with a pair of sunglasses. "Look, I can't stay, I just wanted to firm up our plans for Sunday night."

"Sure!" I wanted to tell him all about my brand-new dress and the wonderful ladies at Simpson's and how excited we all were about the big party. But he seemed impatient to get on his way.

"I'll pick you up in front of your place at nine sharp. Okay?"

Oh. Well, what had I expected? That he would ring the bell and introduce himself to Grady?

I guess I sort of had.

"Sure! For sure. I'm very punctual. I have a new dress."

"Great, gotta run, see you Sunday, babe."

I watched him thread his way through incoming clientele. He was handsome from the back too. Ow. My stomach hurt. I was just tired. Yeah, no sleep and too much happening. That must be why my stomach was cramping.

"Where Did Our Love Go"

(THE SUPREMES)

YOU'RE GONNA STOP traffic!" Grady lit a fresh cigarette. "You're beautiful. You could be going to the prom!"

"Really? Are you sure?"

"Never been surer of anything in my life. Miss Zelda did you up fine." She flicked at an invisible speck on her own outfit. Grady was wearing a shiny black taffeta skirt with a white blouse, all pulled together with a red belt and red high heels.

"And I've never seen you look lovelier, Grady."

She sat on her sofa ever so carefully, so as not to crease the skirt. "I wanted to look especially nice when I meet your young man."

"Oh Grady." I felt myself crumple. "He's not coming in."

"What?" She looked pained. "Why ever not?"

"I'm meeting him outside at nine sharp." Seeing the look on her face, I felt guilt nibbling the edges of my pretty new dress. "It's kind of, well, he's probably coming in a taxi and he'll just have it waiting or something. It's the modern thing, you know?"

"But I'm sober and I haven't met this guy. You've been holding your cards a little too close to your chest on this one, young lady. What are you hiding?"

"Nothing!" But there *was* something. It's just that I didn't know *what*. And that made me angry. "And it's not like you're my mom or Mrs. Hazelton or anything. I don't need your approval, Grady. You're just the landlady!" I tried sucking the words back in as soon as they shot out of my mouth, but they had landed on her. Now I was angry for no good reason and ashamed for a pretty good one.

"Just? Just!"

"Grady, oh God, I'm sorry. I didn't mean that, honest I didn't! I…" I'd insulted her. Worse, I'd hurt her. She was the last person in the world I wanted to hurt. Grady had been nothing but good to me from the moment she opened the door. Weird, yeah, but real good.

"S'okay." She sniffed. "It's the teen years. I've been reading up on it. Your hormones are acting up. I remember hormones. Vaguely. Get me a drink, kid. There's a bottle of scotch on the kitchen counter."

"But you said that—"

"I said I was sober. I didn't say I wasn't drinking. Don't worry, I'm counting 'em." Counting her drinks was the new thing. I didn't know how the system was supposed to work, since she kept the numbers top secret. "Three fingers, two ice cubes, chop, chop! And where are you going? I want the address."

"I don't know exactly." *Do you pour in the three fingers before or after the two ice cubes?* "It's at a Mr. Marcetti's penthouse. I had to ask Rachel what that was." I went to the kitchen to fix her drink. When I came back I twirled for her a couple of extra times. Landlady or not, I *did* want Grady's approval. "Should I have bought high heels?" I'd purchased beige Mary Janes to match my off-white stockings, but the shoes only had a tiny kitten heel.

"Kid, you're perfect, and the shoes are perfect! You're sixteen, not thirty-six. Now get out of here—it's almost nine. And remember, next time he's coming in!"

"Yes, ma'am." I planted a kiss on her perfectly made-up cheek. "Thank you, Grady."

"Ah!" She waved her hand. "Get lost. Have the time of your life, you hear?"

"Yes, ma'am."

She sighed heavily. "Go!"

Just as I stepped outside, a taxi pulled up. Cassidy jumped out and held the door open for me. He smiled, but it didn't reach his eyes. Once we were in the taxi, he stared out the window, seemingly lost in thought. I countered this by not shutting up the whole way to Mr. Marcetti's. I babbled because I was so nervous and because he wasn't saying much and…mainly because he didn't once say that I looked nice.

Grady thought I looked pretty.

Even I thought I looked pretty.

It wasn't a very long cab ride, but we ended up in a part of the city that I didn't know. While chattering nonstop, I formulated a plan. I would make Cassidy so proud and pleased with me at his boss's party that he would find me irresistible, and he would kiss me right then and there, in front of everybody. People would swoon. Genius, right? I was going to be seventeen in a couple of weeks. No way was I turning seventeen without having been kissed, and it would be a showstopper. Tonight would be my magic night, and then I'd write Betty all about it. No more endless pretending and practicing with pillows or the crook of my hand. My first kiss would be spectacular. I would be held and kissed by a handsome man who, let's face it, probably knew how to kiss a girl. And, despite all his extensive kissing experience, once our lips touched he would have to declare that he was besotted with me, and then…well, things got a little fuzzy after that part.

The point is that your first kiss is practically the most important thing in the world. You remember your first kiss for the rest of your life.

That's what all the magazines said.

We got into an elevator, and I got a bit overexcited. I'd never been in an elevator, after all. Cassidy wouldn't let me push the buttons. He didn't seem annoyed as much as preoccupied. Was he sad? Just as we were about to step off the elevator, he grabbed my arm. It was the first time he had touched me since he came to pick me up.

"Look, Toni, I've got a lot of business contacts to talk to tonight, so I'm not going to be by your side every single minute. Mr. Marcetti is real important to me. His guests are real important to me and…"

"I won't let you down, Cassidy. I promise."

"Yeah. Look, this is a big-girl party. Be a big girl okay?"

I was nodding so hard that my earrings jangled.

And then Mr. Marcetti's door opened without us knocking or anything.

Wow! The place looked like something out of a movie. Mr. Marcetti's penthouse was all supermodern and space-age. Lots of low leather sofas without arms, glass and chrome everywhere and pure-white sculptural tables. There was a long bank of windows. Even from the entrance, you could see the rest of the city spread out before us. Wow. Toronto was at our feet, the whole city! I was too excited to move.

There were lots and lots of people, but the room didn't feel crowded.

Oh yeah, and everybody was old. Well, mostly. The men were really old, like in their forties or fifties, but they all seemed to have married much younger women. Some were sort of dancing in an area near the bank of windows, some were cuddling and actually kissing on the big sofas, and some were just talking and laughing and drinking. Everybody was smoking.

"Ah, Cassidy and the delightful Toni!" Mr. Marcetti appeared out of nowhere. I almost didn't recognize him without his sunglasses. "How perfectly charming you look,

Toni. A precious angel." He took my arm. "Come with me. I'd like to introduce you to a particularly important friend of mine. He's the head of St. Martin's Hospital. Cassidy, perhaps you could attend to that other matter?"

Wait! A hospital? What a good idea! What a great place to start. Why had none of us thought of that before? Maybe someone there would know what had happened to my mother. This man would at least be able to tell me if that were possible. Mr. Marcetti was so thoughtful. He led me to one of the smaller sofas. I glanced back at Cassidy and flashed him a major smile to assure him that, despite my nerves and pounding heart, I wouldn't behave like some small-town hick in this fabulous place with all these glamorous people.

Cassidy nodded before he walked away.

He did not smile back.

"Toni, this is, um, John Doe. John, this is Toni. What did I tell you?"

A very large man stood up with some difficulty.

"Your furniture is going to kill me, Marcetti, but your taste"—he looked me up and down—"is exquisite."

I put out my hand. "It's a pleasure, Mr. Doe." He looked flummoxed for a minute and then shook it.

"Well, I'll leave you to it, shall I?" Mr. Marcetti drifted off to his other guests.

"Want a drink, honey?" Mr. Doe snapped his fingers, and a man with a tray bearing cocktails appeared out of nowhere. Mr. Doe snatched up a glass, which I recognized as scotch, no ice, four fingers.

"No, thank you, sir, I don't drink."

He looked perplexed for a moment, and then he turned back to the waiter. "Scare up a Coke, will you?" He stepped closer to me. "So tell me about yourself, pretty Toni." Mr. Doe ran his hand down my arm, and I bit down on my instinct to step back. I was proud of myself for that. Instead, I launched into the point-form version of my story. Well, as point form as I get.

"You're killing me, honey. That's a real good one!" He kept smiling at all the sad bits, which kind of threw me, but I kept at it to the end, because I was in full motor-mouth mode. "Do you think I might find someone at Toronto General to help me?"

"Sure. 1950?" He shrugged. "Hospitals keep records. I'd go to the supervising nurse in the burn unit. The records are off-limits, but she might be able to track down someone who was there." He downed his drink and snapped his fingers again. The waiter appeared with another scotch for him and a glass of Coke for me.

He ran his hand down my arm again. Why would he do that? Again, I didn't pull away. That would be rude, and I had been raised better. "I realize that it's not your hospital, sir, but may I use your name? Only if I need to, of course."

"John Doe? Sure, honey, you can throw it around anyway you want. Marcetti should crank up the air-conditioning. It's hot in here." He wiped his mouth with the back of his hand. "Okay, I've done something for you, so how about you do something for me?"

"Oh certainly, Mr. Doe." A Frank Sinatra song came on right after the Supremes singing "Where Did Our Love Go?" More couples got up to dance. Older people really liked Frank Sinatra. Perhaps he wanted to dance.

"Let's sit. I'd like a smoke." Mr. Doe reached over to a stainless-steel cigarette box that was on the table. They were all the hand-rolled variety. He lit one, inhaled deeply and wordlessly offered it to me.

Eeewww. It had his spit all over it. I prayed that I hadn't made a face. "Thank you, sir, but I don't smoke."

"You're definitely killing me, dollface." He inhaled deeply again. "Sit closer." He patted a spot that was right beside him.

"Oh look, brownies!" I waved to our waiter, whose silver tray was now laden with delicious-looking chocolaty squares. "I love brownies!"

I thanked the waiter and finished the brownie in three bites. I hadn't had one since…since the orphanage. The dark, rich flavor flooded me with happiness and hurt at the exact same time. I reached for another, and Mr. Doe put his hand on mine. "My hunch is that that one will more than do you. Marcetti makes them potent."

Was he worried I was going to get fat?

And then he put his arm around me.

And then I looked around for Cassidy.

And then things got weird.

And then weirder…

"Can't Buy Me Love"

(THE BEATLES)

MR. DOE WAS perspiring. A lot. In fact, he was pretty much gushing. Sweat stains morphed into ponds on his shirt. I couldn't look away. He was also emitting a not-so-faint aroma of wet socks and dog fart. For some reason this struck me as hilarious. I started giggling.

"That's better, honey. How long have you been a party girl?" His forehead was beaded with sweat dots that joined up into delicate rivulets that slid down the sides of his ruddy cheeks. There was just so much happening on him.

"Oh, this is my very first party, Mr. Doe." The streams ran down his face and into the folds on his neck and then back out again. The sweat hypnotized me, held me in place. I'd never really noticed sweat before. It had a life of its own. He moved in a little closer. "Dance?"

"No sir, I've never been to a dance either. Well, of course, the Seven danced all the time. Jumpin' Joe—Lord, I miss him—anyway, Joe would teach me some moves in the kitchen and then, when it was supposed to be lights out, I'd teach the others, and we'd dance and dance until, sure as shooting, that old bat Miss Webster would somehow get wind of it all and then…well, you know, she wasn't all bad, I suppose someone had to impose discipline or we would have run riot. I see that now, most of the time I guess, and…" I was vaguely aware that I wasn't making any sense. Truth was, I wasn't really paying attention to anything I was saying because Mr. Doe kept inching closer.

What if his sweat got on my dress? Where was Cassidy? Why didn't they play some Beatles music? "Can't Buy Me Love" was my new favorite.

Sweaty, sweaty, sweaty.

God.

What was the matter with me? I couldn't hang on to a single thought. There were so many things to think about. Big things, little things, sweat things. So much to look at. I ogled the dancers, who were still swaying to Frank Sinatra, only now the room was swaying with them. Whoa!

I turned back to Mr. Doe, but he was still a one-man geyser and it was making me nauseous, so I stared at his hands instead. Mistake. What hair Mr. Doe lacked on his head he made up for on his hands. Each fat, moist finger had this little tuft of fur on it. His wedding ring looked like it was cutting off his blood supply. The flesh on his finger spilled out above and below the ring.

Wow, that must hurt.

Laughter and the occasional squeal slid through the Sinatra. I was vaguely aware that the two couples sitting on the sofa opposite us were locked in a tight embrace, hands roaming. Like, in front of everyone and everything. I would have been scandalized, should have been, but it was like someone had thrown a soft, fluffy blanket over me, and, and...*where was Cassidy?*

Mr. Doe caught me watching the grappling couples. He launched a hairy, sweat-soaked arm around me and drew me closer. "Come here, honey." He jutted his chins at the embracing couples. "I bet they got you in the mood, huh?"

Huh? What mood? What was he doing? He was sweating all over my dress. Slowly, and much too late, alarm bells started clanging in my head. *Oh no.* I tried to pull back. Couldn't. His grip was too strong.

"Mr. Doe, please!"

"Oh cut the act, honey. Marcetti promised me a good time, and I'm ready to collect."

Mr. Marcetti? I didn't understand. I searched the room for Cassidy. I had to leave, but the sheer bulk of Mr. Doe had me pinned against the back of the sofa. My head cleared in the space of a heartbeat, making room for the panic to take hold.

"Where is she?"

Who was that? Cassidy?

"Come here, baby." John Doe took his big, fat, wet hand and grabbed my jaw, turning my face toward his.

No.

"I said, where is she?"

He pulled me in closer. The invisible fluffy blanket was stripped off and I was *present*. I could feel the breath from his nostrils on my face. He reeked of scotch and decay.

Not like this. Please God, no!

"Toni, you here? Toni!"

He forced my mouth open and put his wet, slippery lips on mine. I almost threw up. *NO!* His right hand shoved the back of my head into his face so I couldn't turn away. His left hand found my knee and then my thigh…The horror of what was happening flooded but did not paralyze me. I somehow found my shoe, grabbed it and smashed Mr. John Doe on the back of his head with my kitten heel.

"Ow! What the…?"

"Toni!"

Ethan had somehow appeared at the sofa. Was I hallucinating?

"Get lost, kid!" Mr. Doe snarled.

More kerfuffle. Ethan was here! Ethan! I was giddy with relief.

I popped up and was yanked right back down. Ethan leaned over to Mr. Doe. "Look, bud, she's a minor and the cops are coming."

Mr. Doe let go of me like I was infected.

The couple across from us disentangled. "Cops?"

"Yeah." Ethan turned and yelled, "Hey, everybody, quick, clear out! The cops are coming!"

Instant chaos. The girls shrieked, and the men reached
for their ties and shoes before they headed for the door.
Mr. Marcetti shouted at everybody to calm down. Then,
pointing to Ethan from across the penthouse, he yelled to
his guys wearing the sunglasses. "Get him!"

But there was too much confusion, too much shrieking,
too many bodies stampeding in the way.

"Toni, over here!" It was Cassidy. My Cassidy, nobody's
Cassidy. What had he done to me? Why? We locked eyes.
He looked disheveled, pained. "Now!" He waved us both
over. "At the back of the kitchen there's a service elevator.
Let's go!" He took off for the far end of the penthouse.
Ethan grabbed my hand and we followed. I glanced back.
Fear and confusion were escalating in the rest of the place.
Distraught partygoers were converging on the entrance
despite Mr. Marcetti's men trying to turn them back.

Cassidy led us through the kitchen. We startled a couple
of caterers. "To the left!" We veered left to a small back
hallway and a couple of doors. "Go through the black door.
There's an elevator to the garage."

"Cassidy?"

"I'm sorry, Toni, I'm sorry. If it helps, I'm done for here.
I'm out. God, Toni, please, I'm..." He reached for me, but
Ethan pulled me away.

"Hands off, jerk!"

Cassidy shook his head. "Go!"

The elevator went straight to the garage, but we had to
run all around the garage to find the doors and then figure

out how to open them. Finally, we broke free. As soon as we got outside, we took off again. I wasn't doing so great with my one kitten heel, but Ethan never let go of me. We didn't stop running until we got to Queen's Park. Just when I thought I'd break in two, Ethan led us to one of the park benches. We both collapsed. It seemed like the longest night of my life, and it was only ten thirty.

What had just happened? How did it happen? I started to shake. Ethan turned to me. "Are you cold?"

"No," I whispered. "No."

"Toni, are you okay?"

Did I shrug while I shook? *Stupid, stupid girl.*

I was gulping down shame in batches so sticky that I couldn't free the words to thank him. I couldn't even look at him.

"Toni, say something, please." His voice was soft, no longer out of breath. "Did he hurt you?"

Did he hurt me? No, but I was hurt. "How did you find me?"

"Big Bob hit the roof!" He shook his head. "I mean, he totally blew up. Thank God you told Grady it was a Marcetti party. Grady didn't know what that meant, but Big Bob sure did." Ethan leaned forward. "Look, apparently the guy is notorious for these kinds of parties, for bringing in pretty paid companions or party girls. One of the guys in the band said that Cassidy is one of his, uh, purveyors. He finds girls for Marcetti."

Thank God it was so dark. Thank God he couldn't see me. Thank God I couldn't see me.

"Big Bob was heading straight for the door when Grady convinced him to call me. See, if Big Bob turned up, it would signal a club war, and Marcetti is connected big-time. It all happened within ten minutes."

I stared at the grass and kicked off my lone shoe. "But you called the police, right? They'll shut it down, right?"

Ethan shook his head. "I didn't call them, Toni. That was a Hail Mary pass on my part. When I say Marcetti is connected, I mean connected. The police may or may not have helped, depending on who responded." He stood up. "He'll have to lay low for a spell and regroup, but he's a cockroach. Indestructible. We better get going." He extended his hands. "If we're not back by eleven, Big Bob and some guys from the club are going to come after us."

"For me? Oh God, I'm so sorry. I'm sorry and stupid and just so…sorry. I thought Cassidy liked me. I don't deserve to breathe." I wanted to crawl into a ditch.

"No, Toni, no. You're just…sweet and trusting and maybe a little naïve. It's not a bad thing." He held my hands. "But I need to know if that man hurt you."

I deserved it. I must have deserved it for being so stupid and blind and…

"Toni, did he hurt you?"

"Why?"

"Because I'll go back and kill him is why."

I held myself and started rocking. "No, not really, no…
but…" The kiss, that slobbering, vile, open mouth, the
smell and the sweat, all that sweat. I lost it.

I wailed so loud that I scared the squirrels.

"What? Toni, what is it? What happened to you?" Ethan
held my arms. "Tell me!"

"He kissed me! I've been waiting my whole life for my
first kiss, my whole life, and *he* kissed me! I dreamed and
dreamed and the…" I started hiccupping. More punish-
ment. I was in a full-on ugly cry that was now accompanied
by embarrassing hiccups. "I'm going to be seventeen *hic* in
a couple of weeks and *hic* I'd never ever been kissed! And I
dreamed…And it was *him!* How *hic* pathetic is that?"

"Oh Toni, shhh…it's okay." Ethan cupped my face in
his hands and wiped away my tears as I continued hiccupping. "I should have done this the moment I saw you. God
knows I wanted to. My mistake." He leaned down and tilted
my head upward. He kissed my forehead and a part of me
calmed down. But another part lit up.

"But…*hic*."

"Shhh." He kissed my cheek as soft as a whisper and
then the other cheek. Even though it was night, Ethan still
smelled of sunlight and coffee.

"May I kiss you, Antoinette Royce?"

I felt his heart beating against my hand. Did I nod as I
hiccuped? I wanted to shout, "Yes, yes, and hurry!"

He pulled me into him and wrapped his arms around
me, and then Ethan Goldman's lips touched mine. It started

gentle and sweet, like kissing velvet. And then he drew me closer. A soft moan escaped from deep within him—or was that me? We fit perfectly. And then he kissed me harder, and then it was even better, and then he didn't stop. And then I couldn't breathe, and it didn't matter. And then I stopped hiccupping.

And then I kissed Ethan Goldman back.

"People"

(BARBRA STREISAND)

I CRIED NONSTOP. And I felt myself turn pink every single time I remembered Ethan kissing me. Basically, I was a crying, blushing machine. Since the Purple Onion was closed on Mondays, I did most of the caterwauling in my room and a bit with Grady, who insisted I come down for a "drink" in the late afternoon. We dismembered the whole sordid Marcetti/Cassidy story bit by bit. She said it would help me see things more clearly. Maybe, but my eyes were pretty fogged up with humiliation. Grady was wildly relieved, and I was wildly mortified. She tried to explain the whole "party girl" thing to me without corrupting my "innocence" any more than she had to.

"But I don't understand Cassidy's part in this," I said in between sniffles. "I thought he liked me!"

"Well, kid…" She got up as if to get a refreshment, thought better of it and sat right back down. "You said he was a real looker, right? Apparently, Marcetti uses pretty boys to prey on pretty girls, vulnerable girls without any real family or people around." She examined her manicure. "And then he sort of convinces them to, uh, work for him at parties. Most of them do it, honey. Word is, your guy has flown the coop though. Maybe you were the straw that broke the camel's back. That's something."

Not much.

When I wasn't crying, wincing or blushing, I reviewed Grady's description of Marcetti's targets: *vulnerable girls, without any people around.* Well, that was me, all right. No people.

I dried up enough to start my shift on Tuesday, but then Rachel teared up as soon as she saw me.

"Rachel, don't you start! Stop this minute. Why are *you* crying?"

"It's called transference," she sniffled. "I read about it in *Cosmopolitan* magazine. Let's face it. I know all about love gone wrong, broken, stomped-on hearts, and every country-and-western-song cliché there is."

"I didn't love him, Rachel."

"Well, praise the Lord for smallish favors."

"But I liked him a whole lot, and, and I thought he liked me. He made me feel special and made me feel…and, well, he listened and he was so handsome and older and…hand-some." I leaned against the espresso machine as I foamed up the milk. "Grady said that he was grooming me as a Marcetti party girl. I am, bar none, the stupidest girl who ever got off a bus."

She took the milk container away from me. I had over-
foamed. "Nah, sweetie, there's plenty dumber than you."
Rachel folded her arms, clearly pleased with offering up
that revelation.

I finished making my cappuccinos without saying
anything more. What would have happened if Ethan hadn't
come after me? I flashed to that sweaty mouth on mine.
I was a little unsteady as I headed off to my customers.
Rachel stepped in behind me. "The shame bits will get
easier, I promise. Eventually, there will be long periods
where you don't even think about it and then boom—you
remember it in a hurting flash and you wince. Then it goes
away again until the next wince." She squeezed my shoulder.
"We all have 'em, Toni. It's part of being a woman, sweetie.
I promise, there's not a girl alive who doesn't have a few."

If I hadn't been holding coffee cups, I would have
hugged her.

Ethan and I didn't get much of a chance to talk for the
rest of the shift. Big Bob was out of town on a talent search,
so Ethan was at front of house and managing the place as
well. But he smiled or winked every time he caught my
eye. Did he just feel sorry for me? Was it a pity kiss? *I bet
it was. Maybe not. I don't know.* I no longer trusted my judgment. How could I?

Then, just before the eleven o'clock set, who should
walk in but Mr. Kenyatta *and* the professor! As far as
I knew, neither of them had ever set foot in the place.
I didn't know about Mr. Kenyatta, but the professor had

always said he'd turn up when the Onion got a liquor license and not a minute before. Ethan directed them to one of my tables. They both seemed a little awkward and more than a bit nervous as I took their orders. That made me so happy. Not that they were nervous, but that I was thinking about something and someone other than myself for a minute. They waved me over after the last set. The weekday crowd had thinned.

Mr. Kenyatta patted the empty seat beside him. "Are you allowed to join us for a moment? It appears that most of your patrons have departed." I waved at Ethan, who was helping the band with their equipment. He nodded at me from onstage.

Mr. Kenyatta, of course, stood up and pulled out my chair.

"I'll have to clean up in a few minutes, but hey, I'm just so happy to see you here."

"And we're both delighted to see you in your place of employment." The professor looked stone-cold sober. I wasn't sure I had ever seen him in that condition before. Then Mr. Kenyatta leaned over to me.

"I have some information, Miss Toni. I have possible dates for a fire that could be your fire. But perhaps this is not the time. Eddy has intimated that you received quite a shock over the weekend."

Of course Grady would've told the professor.

Wait! Eddy?

I tried not to smile.

"The kid's as tough as nails," said the professor. "And she'll get even tougher once she knows what's what. I've heard her have nightmares every night this week."

I shrank in my chair. I'd thought, since he hadn't come down and banged on my door, that he hadn't heard me scream myself awake.

"Toni?"

I nodded at Mr. Kenyatta.

"The newspaper clippings were not that useful in the end, I'm afraid. As you know, there were many fires, and most of them were deliberately set. The papers lost interest, at least when it came to follow-up. There are three significant dates, however, when residents seem to have been involved. The first two involve male occupants. Then there's one on March 16 that took place in a basement; there was an ambulance present."

I cringed.

He patted my hand. "I'm not exactly sure how this date will help you, but…"

"I got out of the hospital a month or so later. That must be the date, Mr. Kenyatta. I'm going to go to Toronto General." I didn't know that until I said it. But there it was. Rachel had drifted over to our little table, and the gentlemen introduced themselves. Then she plopped herself down, still clutching a dishrag and vinegar cleaner.

"So what are you fellas cooking up? Does it involve my girl here? 'Cause personally, I believe that unless it's a picnic, she's been through enough."

The professor, after checking with me, brought her up to speed. When he finished, Rachel shook her head. "So you're just going to march into a big-city hospital with a date and demand to see thirteen-year-old records?"

The "gentlemen" turned to me.

"Well, at the party I met the awful...anyway, he was a hospital administrator, a head guy."

Rachel groaned.

"No, really, and he said if I had a date, I could maybe track down someone who had worked in the burn unit at the time, and they might know the story."

Mr. Kenyatta and the professor both nodded.

Rachel did not. "Yeah, so what was this hospital administrator's name?"

All that oozing sweat and stink. I shuddered. "Mr. John Doe."

Everybody groaned. Rachel hit her head on the table.

"What? What?"

"Sweetie, that's like a placeholder name, a fake. The police use it when they haven't identified the suspect or the victim."

Was there no end to my stupidity?

"Although that is perfectly correct," said the professor, "it does not negate the value of the idea. The idea is a good one." Mr. Kenyatta agreed immediately, which was kind of cute.

"Yeah, okay, I guess she could try." Rachel shrugged. How had she ended up leading this group? "But she's not going in alone. The kid's like a hand grenade—prisons, parties, now a hospital."

"Agreed." Both men nodded.

"But it's *my* story, people!"

"Take Ethan. You've both got a late shift on Friday, so you can spend the whole day prancing around hospital corridors."

Again both gentlemen nodded. They didn't even know who Ethan was, for God's sake. "He's done enough rescuing for one summer, I think," I said.

"Oh *that* Ethan!" The professor was grinning now. Yup, Grady had completely filled him in on my Sunday-night adventure. "Is he the tall young man onstage?"

"Yup! And *that* Ethan"—Rachel was pointing at him, which I felt was completely unnecessary—"is totally, completely smitten with *our* Toni."

Face on fire! Face on fire!

"And the only person in all of Yorkville who doesn't know it is—you guessed it—our Toni. Go ask him!" Rachel crossed her arms. "I'll clean up your station. You go ask him. Go, before I take back my cleanup offer!"

The professor looked grave. "It would be wiser to be with someone who cares, if and when you receive upsetting information."

I was outgunned and outmaneuvered.

"Fine." I got up and dragged my feet across the club and over to the stage. I felt like one of Napoleon's troops on the forced march across the Russian steppes. "Hey."

"Hey." Ethan smiled and extended his hand to help me up onto the stage. It dawned on me that Ethan was always turning up and extending his hand. It couldn't always be out of pity, could it? Was there any truth to what Rachel said? I felt myself light up from tip to toe the moment he touched me.

Why did it happen every time he touched me? It was nerve-wracking.

"What's up?" He put down some sheet music and smiled at me. "You guys looked like you were plotting to overthrow the government or something."

"We were, sort of. They—no, I think it's time to finally put all the pieces together about my mom. Find out whether she was crazy or whether she tried to hurt me, why she gave me up and, I guess most important, whether she's out there somewhere. I need to know if I have any people, you know?"

Ethan stepped toward me. "That's a hell of list. How are you going to find any of that out?"

"There was a fire where my mother and I were living when I was about three. Mr. Kenyatta figured out the date. I believe we were both taken to Toronto General. I think if I go to the burn unit, there may be someone there who would have been around thirteen years ago and maybe they would tell me…I need to know what happened."

What would they tell me? Would they know that she had tried to kill me? *Did* she start the fire?

"Whoa!" Ethan reached for me. "Are you okay? Look, are you sure you're up for this?"

"I am. Look, I know I've been a lot of trouble. I've always been a lot of trouble, even back home, Miss Webster always said so, but would you, I mean, I'll fill you in on everything I know, but if you wouldn't mind, on Friday, do you think that—"

"I'll pick you up at Grady's at ten."

I didn't realize that I'd been holding my breath. "Thank you." I exhaled so deeply that the stage spun.

"And Toni." He pulled me into him. "You *are* a lot of trouble, but you're worth it. You're worth it and every bit more." He swept a strand of hair out of my eyes. I needed to kiss him. "And I, for one, would do anything for you, Toni Royce."

Kiss me, kiss me.

He traced my cheek with his fingers. *Please, just…* Ethan folded me into him with a strength and tenderness that I didn't know was possible as a combination. He reached up and into the back of my hair, tilting my head just before he put his mouth on mine. I threw my arms around him, hard. His kiss was gentler, sweeter and deeper than the last time. But it was just as long, just as forever, and somewhere in the midst of all of that, I swear I heard clapping.

"Don't Let the Rain Come Down"

(THE SERENDIPITY SINGERS)

WE WENT INTO the emergency entrance by mistake and got yelled at by everyone. Hospitals are very, very scary places.

And they stink.

And I wanted to run.

And Ethan wouldn't let me.

After we got thrown out of emergency, we walked all the way around to the other side, to the main entrance. That looked even scarier than the emergency entrance. I didn't want to go in.

"It'll be okay. I'll be with you."

My heart was pounding and my head was buzzing. "Sorry, I don't know why I'm so scared. It's crazy. I'm ready to find out whatever I need to find out. Really, I am. I don't know what's the matter with me."

We were on the outside of doors that whooshed open and shut all by themselves. Okay, not all by themselves.

Apparently, you had to stand in a certain spot and then they just opened and shut by themselves. We made that discovery when we figured out that where we were standing was causing all the whooshing. Weird, scary, scary place.

Ethan pulled me away from the crazy doors. "Toni, look, are you maybe remembering stuff from when you were three, from when they brought you here, and, well, they wouldn't be good memories, right?"

"No." I started vibrating. "No, I don't remember anything." But that was a lie. It was like scenes from a movie started playing in my head the moment I stepped into emergency. All that screaming, the pain, so much screaming. Was that me?

"*Mommy, I want my Mommy! MOMMY!*"

"*Hold her down.*"

"*Mommy!*"

"*Restrain her, damn it! IV fluids stat! We have to extract this...*"

"*MOMMY!*"

"*Ketamine stat.*"

"Why would I call out for her?"

Ethan drew me closer. "What? You do remember something, don't you?"

"Ethan, I was screaming for my mother. My mother, for God's sake! It hurt so bad. Glass shards stuck all over me, blood everywhere. Doctors and nurses rushing all around, poking me, yelling. But why would I call out for her? She's the one that hurt me. I remember that clearly now. It's not a dream."

"I don't know, Toni." He put his arms around me. We must've looked like a grieving couple. I didn't stop shaking even as he held me. "We don't have to do this." He kissed the top of my head.

"And you wouldn't think worse of me?"

He kissed my forehead. "Look, I'm a goner. I was the moment I saw you mooning over Ian Tyson's playbill outside the club."

I smacked him.

"But you acted like you couldn't stand the sight of me."

"Me? I did not..."

"And then there was Tyson, and then you thought I was your brother, for God's sake! So I told myself it didn't matter. But it did, Toni."

"But it wasn't true! I just got all confused in my search..."

"And then...then there was the old guy." I felt rather than heard him growl.

"I thought he cared. That finally somebody cared. I was so flattered and thrilled and...stupid," I mumbled into his chest.

"I was the stupid one, Toni. I should have known better. Everything was too new and overwhelming for you those first few weeks. I couldn't wrap my head around that because my bruised ego got in the way." He caressed my cheek. "I should have stepped up, but instead I stepped away. But I'm here now, and I'll do whatever you need me to do."

I knew what had to happen. "Let's go in."

The doors whooshed open, but this time we stepped through them. Ethan walked right up to the information desk as if he did this sort of thing every day. "Burn unit, please."

An old biddy at the desk stopped chewing on a Snickers bar long enough to look at him suspiciously. "Family member?"

"Yes, ma'am." Ethan nodded. "We're here to see about her mother."

Well, it was true.

She eyed us both. "Seventh floor. Turn right and keep going until you get to the supervising desk, and one of the nurses will see to you. Do *not* try going into any of the unit rooms, hear?"

"No, ma'am." Scary, scary place. "Thank you, ma'am."

In some ways, it was worse than the prison. All the doors to the rooms were closed, and we couldn't see anything. But the noises were bad. The sound of machines—compressing, beeping—intruded into the hushed bubble of the ward. Worse were the pitiful, heart-wrenching little moans escaping from some of the closed rooms.

But none of it looked familiar to me.

When we reached the nurses' station, a formidable-looking nurse greeted us as if were invading sacred ground.

"What are you kids doing here?"

"Please, ma'am," I started before Ethan could jump in and save me. It was my quest, after all. "I'm looking for some very important information. I believe my mother may have been in this burn unit in 1950." The nurse tapped her nails against the desk faster and faster, seeming to get more irritated with every word. "Please, I just want—need—some information. I need to know what happened to my mother."

"Does this look like social services? Who let you up here?"

I felt Ethan tense behind me.

"No, ma'am," I continued. "But I was here too, and I was released on April 30 to an orphanage, and I have no idea—"

"Listen." She raised her hand. "For starters, we didn't even have a burn unit in the fifties. Nobody did. Burns were treated in the general surgical wards, and it was far grimmer than it is now. It's still no place for a couple of curious kids to be traipsing around."

It felt like one of the medical machines was sucking all the air out of my lungs. I steadied myself on the counter, trying to gather myself. I read the name tag on her uniform. "Please, Nurse Hamilton." Individual smells began to invade me. I could pick out the stench of wet bandages and raw tissue through that of Clorox and urine. "I can tell that you're far too young to have been working here then, but if you could just direct me to a doctor who might have been on the surgical ward at the time, well, he might remember.

I know I can't look at records or anything like that, but please, I need to know what happened to me."

Nurse Hamilton patted her silver hair, which was every bit as starched as her cap. She looked around as if checking for interlopers. "As it turns out, I was around then. Dr. Marsden, who is the current head of the burn unit, was a resident around that time."

"That's great!"

She shook her head. "He's on vacation for the rest of the month at his cottage. There's no reaching him, and there's going to be no nosing through records, if that's what you're secretly hoping."

"Oh, I—"

"So, what is your mother's name?"

"It is, or was, Halina Royce."

Did she flinch? She certainly turned away. When she turned back, she sized me up full on.

"Nurse Sanchez is Dr. Marsden's right arm and was from the beginning." She sighed heavily at the console in front of her. "She's on the ward now. We don't allow them to take vacations at the same time, see?"

I didn't, but I nodded.

Nurse Hamilton seemed to be having a private conversation with herself while I stood there silently willing her to help me. She sighed again, leaned into the console and pushed a button. "Nurse Sanchez to the front desk. Nurse Sanchez stat."

Within seconds one of the doors down on the east hall opened and then closed. I heard her before I saw her.

It seemed that all the nurses' shoes either squeaked or creaked. Nurse Sanchez was an explosion wrapped in a white uniform. Her glossy black hair was pulled and pinned to within an inch of its life under her cap, and still rebellious strands escaped. Her complexion was the color of café au lait, her lips were a shade of red that would have made Grady proud, and you could feel the annoyance wafting off her.

"Nurse Hamilton?"

"Nurse Sanchez." Nurse Hamilton waved her reading glasses in our general direction. "This young woman needs your help. She is looking for information. Burn victims at the beginning of your career. A mother and daughter, March 1950. Perhaps you could direct them to someone."

Nurse Sanchez turned to me, but her expression didn't change. I'd never seen eyes that were blacker or more beautiful. "Name?"

"My mother was the burn victim. I just had cuts, glass shards that were—"

"Name?" she repeated.

"Sorry. My mother's name was—is—Halina Royce. I'm Toni, Antoinette Royce, ma'am."

The nurses exchanged a long glance.

"Room 2B is free." Nurse Hamilton nodded. "I'll have an orderly sent to Mr. Visinsky's room until you return." She studied a heavily marked-up floor plan.

Nurse Sanchez turned to us. "Follow me." Was she less annoyed?

We padded behind her down an endless corridor. Every moan I heard reverberated in my bone marrow; every beep and mechanical hiss vibrated in my gut. Did she know anything? How could she work in this place of pain? How could anyone work here? No wonder she was angry. After going past at least a thousand rooms, we reached a door at the very end of the corridor. She led us into a window-less gray room with four mismatched and randomly placed chairs, a gurgling water cooler and a very large plant that looked like it didn't care whether it lived or died.

"Sit."

We sat. "Thank you for seeing us, Nurse Sanchez. I don't mean to annoy or pester you, but I just need...if you know who took care of us, of me, it would be, well, it's incredibly important that I figure some things out."

Nurse Sanchez turned to us. She pulled out a chair and sat directly in front of me. Her dark eyes glistened. "It was me, Antoinette, me. I was your nurse."

"You? Oh..." And just like that, there it was, the end of my quest.

"I can't believe that no one told you. Are you sure you're ready to hear?"

"Yes, ma'am." I nodded. "Yes, for sure I am."

But I wasn't. I was nowhere near ready.

"Rag Doll"

(THE FOUR SEASONS)

I NEVER THOUGHT I'd see you again." She shook her head. "But I wondered, we've all wondered, what happened to you. Dr. Marsden was the resident on call, and you, Antoinette, were close to being my very first patient. None of us will ever forget." Nurse Sanchez looked to the gray walls, clearly seeing something other than scuffs and peeling paint. "That old warhorse at the front desk surely remembers. It's the only reason you weren't thrown out. But, yes, I was your nurse."

She smiled at me. "You're beautiful. I can't see any…"

"No," I said, "they're faded and smaller, but they're all over my body. A couple here." I pulled down my turtleneck and craned my neck just so.

"You're so beautiful," she repeated. "It's a miracle. If you could have seen yourself, well, good thing you couldn't. Dr. Marsden did good initial work on you, before the surgeries." She nodded approvingly.

Surgeries? Plural?

Unlike the rest of the ward, the room we were in wasn't air-conditioned. Perspiration raced down my back.

"One of the shards struck your spleen. The blood loss was...and, well, of course, your little body was just covered in blood, slick with it. Not your face. Apparently, your mother covered your face with a towel. You almost suffocated."

She tried to suffocate me too? I couldn't go there. The air got thicker, making it more difficult to catch a clear breath. "I'd like to know about my mother."

"What do you know so far?" she whispered. Why was she whispering?

"Nothing!" Did I yell? Ethan put his arm around me. I shook it off and continued yelling. "I don't know anything! I was taken to an orphanage, and they don't know or wouldn't tell and I have these dreams...Is she alive somewhere? I mean, I know you wouldn't know where, and I don't want to get you in trouble, but I don't know anything. Zero, zilch! Please..."

The water cooler came to life, gurgling so aggressively that we all turned to confront it.

"I'm still not entirely sure that I should be the one to..." She turned back to me. "How could they not have told you?"

"Well, they didn't!" Ethan shot out of his chair. "It's crazy! She's been racing around the city, begging for clues, but she doesn't know hardly anything about herself!

And that's just not right. It's 1964 not 1864. Could you please just tell her what you know."

Nurse Sanchez seemed to be collecting herself. She did not look at me. "She died here, Antoinette."

Died?

"Toni. I'm called Toni," I said for no good reason. There seemed to be a faint, low buzz in the room.

Died…

My mother had been dead all these years. But I knew that. Really, I did. Deep in the darkest and ugliest part of my secret self—I knew. I always knew. Was that why I never allowed myself to pretend along with the Seven?

"Your mother succumbed to her injuries eight days after she was admitted." Nurse Sanchez leaned over and rested her arms on her knees. "We didn't know things back then like we do now, but I believe she wouldn't have survived her injuries even today, even in the burn unit. It was…she was too…it was over 80 percent of her body."

Did she try to kill herself? Kill us both? Was that it? My stomach felt like someone was wringing it out like a wet towel. "Did you—did anyone figure out if she was the one who set the fire?"

She turned sharply. "What? No! Oh, dear Lord, no. It was the owner. The police were all over us and her, looking for a statement. They never got it. She couldn't remember anything, so he was never charged." The nurse scrubbed her face with her hands. "I don't think that either of you were supposed to be in the building at the time, but you were sick with a cold, so your mother stayed at home with you. We got that much. He was some small-time punk who owned a couple of buildings. Both of them were torched. The first one was just three weeks before. For the insurance money." She got up and went to the gurgling water cooler and filled a tiny paper cone with water.

The cone was a thing of wonder. Why didn't it leak? It was only paper, after all. Why didn't it leak? The buzzing got louder, or was it a hum?

"No one got hurt in his first fire." Nurse Sanchez crushed the cup and tossed it clear across the room. It hit the rim of the wastebasket and landed on the floor. No one moved. "We didn't even get your full names for days after. The identification was in the building. She was just clutching a couple of pieces of paper, and they went to—"

"The orphanage? It must have been the playbill and the menu."

"Perhaps. Those papers and your release went with you when you left. Your mother wasn't lucid enough most of the time before she..."

"Died." I finished for her.

"Yes. It was a hard passing. I'm sorry, Antoinette, Toni, but it was. Nurse Hamilton never saw anything like it, and she was as tough as nails even back then. Your mother wouldn't let go, despite unbearable pain." Nurse Sanchez sat down again. "She should have passed that first night. We stopped procedures, but she hung on and on." Nurse Sanchez clasped her hands. "You have no idea what burn victims go through. But she wanted to pull through for you, Toni. That's what Nurse Hamilton said. She had her for five shifts straight. The woman is a concrete wall, but there's none better."

I yanked my head out of the tunnel it was in. "For me?" But that didn't make sense.

"She called and cried for you nonstop. They couldn't calm her unless they knocked her right out, and she hated being knocked out, despite the agony. It tormented everyone on the floor." Nurse Sanchez stood up again and walked over to the ambivalent plant, eyeing it like it was an intruder.

"The thing is, we were forbidden to bring you into the critical-care unit of the surgical ward. It was absolutely against the rules. Not only that, but you were in bad shape yourself after the surgeries and all that stitching up." She slid her fingers over the plant's few decaying leaves. "But it was crippling the floor. Her...situation touched us all. They couldn't calm her. Your poor mom only got more and more agitated and desperate. They told her, promised her, that you were alive, but it did no good. As soon as she got out from under the latest drug load, she'd cry out for you. It got worse every day, every hour..."

I wrapped my arms around myself and started to rock. None of this made sense. Nurse Sanchez's story did not line up with any of my own charred memories.

"So one night, Nurse Hamilton and I arranged the whole thing. Dr. Marsden was off duty, and the other resident was too scared of Nurse Hamilton to be a problem. I took you out of your bed, still attached to the IV pole. You really were a wee little thing. Anyway, I brought you and the pole to the surgical ICU window. Nurse Hamilton and an orderly moved her bed around and cranked it up as high as it would go. The pain must have been excruciating, but your mom wouldn't let them stop." She turned away from the plant. Tears slid quietly down Nurse Sanchez's face. "I held you up as high as I could, and you put your bandaged little hands against the window. And...and your mom tried to raise her hand. She looked...it was..." Nurse Sanchez put her head in her hands. "I don't know how you weren't terrified at the sight of her, but you didn't recoil. It was unbelievable. Somehow you knew her, knew it was still your mom under all of that. Oh God, what a sight."

Ethan, who had been pacing, sat back down.

"You kept calling out, 'Mommy, mommy,' and wriggled like the devil trying to get to her. Your mother wasn't able to smile, but she kept her hand right up and trying to wave, trying to reassure you. I can't imagine what it cost her. 'I want to go home, Mommy!' I can still hear you in my head. She even tried to nod, she really did. And then you cried, and Lord knows we cried right along with you."

There was a knock on the door, and we all started. Nurse Hamilton stepped inside and then thought better of it. "I just wanted to check in."

Ethan produced a fairly clean handkerchief and handed it to Nurse Sanchez, who quickly wiped away her tears.

"I see," sighed Nurse Hamilton. "Does the child remember any of it?"

They turned to me. No, "the child" did not. How could I not? I was wracked with guilt that I didn't. "No," I whispered. "I don't remember."

Nurse Hamilton nodded. Just before she closed the door again, I heard her say, "Just as well. It's just as well."

The interruption gave Nurse Sanchez a moment to compose herself. "I brought you back, kicking and screaming." She smiled at the memory. "Your mother passed that night, as peacefully as she could. She was just waiting. Nurse Hamilton understood that. Your mom just needed to see you, to know that you'd live." Nurse Sanchez sighed. "Nobody knew, or if they did, they didn't talk. It stayed a secret. I don't think I've ever done anything as important in all the years since."

It was a story. Just a story. It was a story about a little girl and her mother and a fire. Like the story Scarlet Sue had told. Now the buzzing was in my head, like an electric wire. Oh sure, it was a tragedy, I got that, but still, it was just a story. It didn't touch me now, not really. It couldn't. I might as well have been reading it from one of the professor's books.

Still, I had questions about this story. I wanted to ask them, but my lips kept getting stuck to my teeth. I had to keep licking them and sliding my tongue around before the words, one by one, broke free.

"But then...see...it doesn't make sense. I...don't understand. Why did she try to kill me? She hurt me...

the glass. I can remember it piercing. I can hear the glass shattering. I *remember* that part. That part is true!"

Nurse Sanchez stared at me in stark astonishment. Her hand flew to her chest. "Oh, dear Lord, Toni, no! She only suffered through that hell for you. Your mother *saved* your life."

"But the glass shattered and—"

"Because she shattered it to get you out!" Nurse Sanchez gripped the arms of the chair as if to hold it in place. "We knew that from the firemen. They said you were in a basement flat with only a small window at street level, high above the floor. Apparently, the fire started in the furnace room and broke through the walls fast. Your mother kept throwing a toaster at the window until it began to shatter, but it wasn't fast enough. Toni, she put a towel over your face, got on a chair and used your body to finish the shattering, and then she shoved you through it, all torn up, just before she succumbed to smoke inhalation."

"Stay still! Tight like a ball!"

I was right. I was wrong.

Ethan walked over to the water cooler and offered Nurse Sanchez another cup of water, which she accepted. "It's over. Don't you see, Toni? She did do it—she hurt you." He said it with a gentleness I didn't know anyone possessed. "But she did it to get you out."

I could barely hear him, the buzzing in my head was so loud.

"He's right. She used up everything she had. That's what the fireman said." Nurse Sanchez nodded. "They couldn't get to her in time."

The universe overturned so violently I thought I'd pass out. I was unmoored. Black was white and up was down. My mother had *saved* my life by sacrificing her own. *My mother held on in unendurable pain until she saw that I was safe.* I had hated her for almost fourteen years.

Who was the monster now?

I can't.

I won't.

I did.

I ran.

I bolted from the chair before either of them could blink.

I ran down the long, long corridor. I passed the elevators—too slow—and ran down seven flights of stairs, tripping through tears and gasping until I got outside to run some more. I ran and I ran and I ran and still could not outrun myself.

I never could.

"Everybody Loves Somebody"

(DEAN MARTIN)

ETHAN CAUGHT UP to me by Wellesley Street, as I was tearing across Queen's Park.

"Whoa! Whoa, whoa!" He grabbed my arm and yanked me to a full stop. "Hey, it's okay, it's okay. Hey!" He looked around the park. "This is fast becoming *our* spot."

I saw his lips move and even recognized some words, but they bounced off me. None of it penetrated. By the time Ethan got to me, I was hysterical.

He tried covering me with his arms and it didn't help; I was keening enough to draw a little crowd.

"It's okay, Toni, it's okay. Don't you see?" He held tight, rocking me, repeating over and over again that it was all right. "You were practically a baby. The important thing is, your mother loved you. She loved you so much."

Or something like that.

I don't remember how we got home.

Did I finally shut up?

I remember Grady was as pale as a sheet. Ethan talked to her. A lot.

She insisted I swallow a finger of brandy. I think I did, and then Grady pulled out a pillow and placed it and me on her sofa.

"I'll be right here. You're not going anywhere and neither am I."

Or something like that.

I think the professor dropped in at some point, but I can't be sure.

I fell asleep while it was still light outside. It was the sleep of the dead, deep and dark and long. I didn't wake up until noon the next day.

There were no dreams.

When I woke up, Grady was in her customary position in her wingback. Her hair was in rollers. She had a mud mask on and was carefully applying a fresh coat of nail polish to her fingernails. "Well, good morning, sleepyhead. I don't know what everybody's talking about. Not only did you not scream your head off, but you didn't budge all night."

How did she know?

I raised myself cautiously. No more buzzing. My head was remarkably clear and I was, remarkably, still exhausted. "Grady, I want to—"

"Yeah, yeah, you want to thank me. Consider it done. Ethan told me the whole story." She whistled. "Hope it wasn't some kind of secret. Kid, you make my life look like a beige wall."

I shook my head and started to get up. "I've got early shift today…"

"Nah, not today you don't. Today you recuperate and cry some more and sleep some more. Rachel and Ethan are covering for you. Sit down."

I sat.

"Tell me all about it from the beginning, right from what Scarlet Sue laid on you onward. I've got coffee brewing." She blew on her nails.

"But I thought that Ethan told you."

"Yeah, he did and now you have to, all of it. Get it out in one long lump, including how you think you're a monster."

I winced. That must have slipped out when I went all hysterical in the park.

"Come on, let's get at it. I just got to warn you, if you start blubbering I'm not going to run over and hug you. First, because I'm not the hugging type, and second, because I'm going to start in on my feet now." And with that warning, Grady started weaving long puffy cotton ropes between her toes. "Go!"

And I did.

I talked for the rest of the afternoon. Grady made pots of coffee and brought in scones. At some point she had to wash off the mud mask, which had dried to the consistency of a sidewalk. In between all that, I talked and Grady asked questions and I talked some more. A lot more. She may not have been the hugging type, but in the end she was a crier.

And she didn't have a single drink. Well, at least not until 5:05 PM, when I got up and made her a scotch, two fingers, no ice.

"Thanks," she said when I handed it to her. "You're a good kid."

I sat by her on the footstool. Grady's toenails had dried hours ago. "Actually, I don't much feel like a kid anymore, Grady. I'm going to be seventeen in a few days, and I feel forty."

"Hey! What the hell's wrong with forty?"

"Nothing! You know what I mean. It's just that, I don't know, it's like I've lived more in almost four months here than I did in almost fourteen years at the orphanage."

"Yup, ready or not." Grady nodded gravely. "You're not a kid anymore, kid."

ℰ

I slowly found my footing over the next few days. Everyone was weirdly gentle with me except for Ethan. Ethan teased me in public and kissed me in private. Each and every kiss seemed to heat through my lips and shoot to every single part of my body. His touch made me nervous and excited at the same time. I didn't know what was going on with me when I was near him.

Away from Ethan, walking the streets of Yorkville or trying to do work on the correspondence course that the professor had lined up for me, I felt alone. And that's because I was. I wasn't all weepy about it. Facts were facts. I *was* alone. I had no family, no people who were *my* people. There wasn't *maybe* someone out there, good or bad, whom I belonged to. The *maybe* was done. It wasn't as bad as it sounds. I knew where I stood.

But I once had a mother who loved me fiercely.

I had been wrong about her, and I was trying to forgive myself for that.

She loved me and that was no fantasy.

On Monday, Grady had me tearing around the city on errands. I was happy to do them for her; no kin could have been better than she was. So I went to Simpson's to buy her three pairs of Hanes nylon stockings. Of course, I paid my respects to Mrs. Howland and Miss Zelda and sidestepped as best I could the "success" of the party.

The party. Rachel was right. An image would flash before me out of nowhere. My stomach would instantly contract and I'd cringe, afraid that other people could see what I had just seen. And then it would just leave.

I would try to learn how to live with that too.

After Simpson's I had to go to a specialty shop in Bloor West, which was at the other end of the city, for these special salamis that Big Bob apparently had a hankering for. And apparently, Grady cared deeply about what Big Bob was hankering for.

I didn't get in until almost six o'clock. "Grady, I'm back!"

"Did you get the salamis?"

"Yes, ma'am."

"Set them on the dining-room table, will you?"

The dining-room table? I had to push open the door with my hip, and as soon as I did, the top of my head blew off.

"SURPRISE!!!!!!!"

The salamis and the nylons tumbled to the floor. The dining room was filled to bursting.

"Happy birthday to you…"

Grady was at the head of the table, with Big Bob at her right. Rachel was crying on his right.

"Happy birthday to you…"

Mr. Goldman was beside her. And the professor and Mr. Kenyatta were across from them. Both of them were seriously off-key.

"Happy birthday dear Toni…"

And singing louder than anyone was Ethan, on Grady's immediate left.

"Happy birthday to you!"

Everyone clapped and hooted. They were all wearing ridiculous party hats, made even more ridiculous by the fact that they were emblazoned with glitter lettering that read *Happy New Year 1959.*

"Blow out your candles!" they chanted.

"It's your birthday and we're going to start with cake!" Grady yelled above the hubbub. "Blow 'em out, kid." It was the biggest, most beautiful birthday cake I had ever seen. Actually, other than on TV or in the movies, I'd never seen a birthday cake, but this one was for sure more glamorous than any of those.

There were eighteen lit candles in between the pink *HAPPY BIRTHDAY TONI* lettering. Ethan said that there was always one extra for luck. I blew them out to thunderous applause and then sat down at the other end of the table from Grady. We started with cake and ice cream and then worked our way backward, through beef stroganoff and butter noodles and salad and back to cake again. The adults got a bit over-refreshed. Even Mr. Kenyatta was tipsy. I could tell because he allowed the professor to hold his hand. Everyone's hats were askew by the time we finished the noodles.

I had a lot to write Betty about.

Mr. Goldman lit into jazz standards with the second round of cake. He belted out "Ain't Misbehavin'" and "The Birth of the Blues" like he had Jumpin' Joe's spirit deep inside him. Ethan joined in on "Mack the Knife," and by the time he swung around to Dean Martin's "Everybody Loves Somebody," we were all singing. As soon as we hit the last note, Ethan jumped up and kissed me, right then and there. And it was a showstopper. The birthday guests whistled and hooted.

I guess it was official. This had been the best and worst year of my life.

Ethan put his arm around me as I tried to make sense of it all and of the people at this crazy table. Big Bob was flexing his right arm, showing off a brand-new tattoo, and Grady squealed like a schoolgirl. The professor and Mr. Kenyatta were still holding hands even as they ate their cake. Mr. Goldman was drumming on the table and trying to tell us that Scarlet Sue would be out by November. Rachel was wailing anew. Apparently, her latest, greatest new fella had flown the coop. What would Joe think of them when he came?

He'd love them. Like I did.

They were a loud, weird, motley mess of people.

But they were my people.

And that was enough.

ACKNOWLEDGMENTS

I must begin by thanking my family, Ken, Sasha and Nikki Toten, who should by now be demanding payment for services rendered as critical first readers. Then there's my delightful fellow partners in crime—Kelley Armstrong, Kathy Kacer, Marthe Jocelyn, Vicki Grant, Norah McClintock and, of course, Eric Walters—extraordinary colleagues and writers all. As always, The Goup—Nancy Hartry, Loris Lesynski, Susan Adach and especially Ann Goldring—did a lot of heavy lifting. Immense gratitude to Sarah Harvey, Andrew Wooldridge and the team at Orca for their ingenuity, patience and, dare I say, fortitude. And, finally, to the city as it was, Toronto 1964. Toronto's history, tragedy and exuberance shaped Toni's story as well as my own.

TERESA TOTEN is the author of the acclaimed Blondes series, as well as *The Game, The Onlyhouse* and, with Eric Walters, *The Taming*. Teresa has been nominated three times for the Governor General's Literary Award and won it in 2013 for *The Unlikely Hero of Room 13B*, which also won the Ruth and Sylvia Schwartz Children's Book Award and the CBC Bookie Award, was the CLA Honour Book for 2013 and was nominated for the 2014 TD Canadian Children's Literature Award. For more information, visit www.teresatoten.com.

Uncover more Secrets—
starting with this excerpt from:

TESS WOKE TO complete darkness. Her arms shot out, heart pounding, certain she would flail against the sides of a wooden box and hear the skitter of dirt. But when she leaped up, nothing stopped her. Nothing except a screaming pain in her head that forced her to her knees as she doubled over, heaving and gagging. She lifted one hand to her head and gingerly prodded a rising bump.

Knocked out. She'd been knocked out and thrown into…

She inhaled the stink of mustiness and felt the dirt beneath her fingers.

A basement. She'd been knocked unconscious and thrown into a basement.

There'd been a man. She remembered running though the woods, trees lashing at her, vines catching her feet. Then a cry. A fall.

She'd fallen? No…She squeezed her eyes shut and focused on the memory. *He'd* fallen. Then she'd escaped, and there'd been a house.

A house…

A house and a broken window and a ladder. Books. Falling. Rotted floor.

No one had thrown her in the basement. She'd fallen.

Tess exhaled so suddenly that her stomach heaved again. She gagged. Then she sat back on her haunches and kept breathing deeply, getting her bearings.

Not kidnapped. Not knocked out. Well, yes, knocked out, but only by her own stupidity. All she had to do was find the stairs and get back to the main floor.

She needed the flashlight. And her purse. The first, though, would help find the second, so she searched on the dirt floor. The flashlight was light gray, which should have made it easier to find than the dark purse, but she spotted the bag first, lying in a heap not far from where she'd fallen. She took it and blinked hard, trying to see better. A little light seeped through the hole in the floor overhead. Very little, given that it was only moonlight shining through the library windows.

Tess looked up at the hole…and saw the flashlight teetering on the edge.

She took a deep breath. No matter. She could fix this.

Tess felt around on the floor and picked up a chunk of fallen wood. She positioned herself under the hole and pitched the wood up at the flashlight. Her aim was perfect.

The wood hit the flashlight…and knocked it backward out of sight.

Tess responded with every swear word she knew. While she was certain Mrs. Hazelton would disagree, there seemed a time and a place for profanity. A purpose too. It certainly made her feel better.

She squared her shoulders and marched forward…only to stumble over a piece of debris. All right then. Less confidence, more caution. She walked slowly, each foot sweeping the way before touching down. She kept her hands outstretched too, and after no more than five steps she felt concrete. A wall. *See, that was easy.* All she had to do was walk—carefully— along the wall until her fingers found the door.

She was at the first corner when she heard scratching. She froze. Silence. She lifted a foot. Another scratch, long and deliberate. Then another. Tess's mind fell back into that nightmare place, trapped in the box, oxygen almost gone, her fingers bloody and raw, the final slow scratches against the wooden—

She shook herself hard. It was a rat. Maybe even just a mouse, but she would accept the possibility of rats. She'd helped Billy when a few got into the storage shed where his parents kept their flour. One swift kick had sent them scattering so Billy could lay out the traps. Rats, she'd realized, were much more frightening in fiction than in reality.

She tilted her head and listened to the scratching. It came from the other side of the wall. *Good enough.* Forewarned was forearmed. *Just find the door. Find the stairs. Get out.*

As she felt her way along the next wall, the scratching stopped. A sob echoed through the room. Every hair on Tess's body shot up, and she strained to hear, telling herself she'd misheard, she *must* have misheard...

Another sob, so clear now that it sounded as if it came from directly behind her. She wheeled, turning her back to the wall. A sniffle. Then crying. Quiet, muffled crying. From the very room where she stood.

"H-hello?"

No one replied. Did she expect an answer? Did she *want* one? No. For the first time in her life, she heard a voice in the dark and prayed it *was* her imagination. Her madness. Because the alternative...

"*Aidez-moi.*" Help me.

No. No, no, no... Tess rubbed her arms as hard as she could. Pain blazed when she touched her skinned elbow, but she didn't care.

"*Aidez-moi,*" the voice whispered. "*S'il vous plaît.*" Help me, please.

Tess wasn't alone down here, and if she wasn't alone, then that meant...

She thought of the branch covering the broken window. Of the flashlight stored there. Of the blanket and pop bottles inside. Of the smell of smoke from the fireplace, and the footprints, all from one set of shoes. It wasn't a group of kids having a bonfire. It was one person.

A man living above. A woman down here.

Every lurid article from every lurid magazine that Tess wasn't supposed to read flooded back to her now. Tales of women held hostage by crazed killers. Those stories always frightened her more than any monster novel, because monsters weren't real. Not the ones with fur and fangs. Human monsters? They were real, and she'd only needed to read a couple of these stories to know they were not her idea of entertainment.

Was it the man from the truck? Surely two men in the same village could not be kidnapping women. Somehow, in escaping him, she'd come straight to his lair. She had no idea how that was possible, but there seemed no other explanation.

"Hello?" she said. Then, "*Où êtes-vous?*" Where are you? A silly thing to ask, but she did anyway.

"*Aidez-moi.*"

"I will. Just…say something else." Tess started forward, her feet sweeping again. She repeated the words in French—or as near an approximation to them as she could manage.

"*Aidez-moi.*"

Tess followed the sound of the voice as she told the woman to keep talking.

"*Je suis désolée.*" I am sorry.

The voice came from near floor level, right in front of Tess. She crouched and reached out. The woman started crying again…behind her.

Tess went still. "*Où êtes-vous?*"

Soft crying answered…from her left now.

"*Je suis désolée. Je suis désolée. Je suis désolée.*"

Each time, the voice came from another direction. Tess rose, her eyes wide and heart pounding as she backed up until she hit the wall.

"*Aidez-moi, s'il vous plaît. Je suis désolée.*" Help me, please. I am sorry.

The words repeated from every corner of the room, getting louder each time, until Tess shrank, crouching, with her hands over her ears.

"Not real. Not real. Not real."

The voice stopped. Tess straightened slowly, one hand clutching her purse strap as if she could use it as a weapon.

A weapon against phantasms? Against her imagination? Against madness?

She gritted her teeth and resumed her methodical circuit around the room. When the crying started again, her fingers shook, but she kept going. One wall, two walls, three walls…four? She'd reached the fourth corner, which meant she'd gone all the way around and failed to find a door.

That wasn't possible. Simply wasn't. Not all rooms were quadrilaterals. She kept going. Fifth wall. Sixth? Seventh? No, that couldn't be. Then her foot struck the same board she'd encountered on the third wall, and she realized she was going around a second time.

Four walls. No exit.

Impossible. She moved more slowly now, her hands reaching down for cubbyholes and up for hatches. There would be something. There had to be.

There was not.

No door. No cubby. No hatch.

"*Aidez-moi, s'il vous plaît. Je suis désolée.*"

Tess clapped her hands over her ears. No doors? Fine. There was a hole in the ceiling, wasn't there? And debris below. If she could pile it and climb—

Footsteps sounded on the floor overhead. Slow, heavy footsteps.

⁕

TESS MOVED AWAY from the hole in the ceiling and huddled in the corner farthest from it as she listened to the footfalls.

"*Qui est là?*" a voice said from above. Who's here?

A male voice. Not a child's but not old enough to be the man in the truck.

"*Il y a quelqu'un?*" Is someone there? Then a grunt, as if in disgust, the voice growing stronger now as he said in French, "I *know* someone's here. You took my flashlight. Come out," followed by something she couldn't translate.

The footsteps stopped. A clatter. The flashlight turned on. A curse then. Or she presumed from his tone that it was a curse, though such vocabulary had not been part of their French lessons.

A thump. A dark figure appeared over the hole. He shone the light straight down at first, as if looking for a body. Then he moved it aside, and she saw a boy, her age or a little older. Straight dark hair fell around his face as he leaned over the edge of the hole. He wore a denim jacket, frayed at the collar and cuffs. In one hand he held the flashlight. In the other...

He moved the beam, and it glinted off a switchblade. Tess shrank back and held her breath, but as soon as he shone that light around the small room...

"*Merde*," he muttered and eased back onto his haunches with a deep, aggrieved sigh. Then he leaned forward again and spoke rapid-fire French. It was clearly a question. When she didn't reply, he said it again, and Tess decided that whatever the situation, cowering wasn't going to help.

She rose and brushed herself off. "Do you speak English?"

"Not if I can help it." His English was thickly accented but much better than her French, so she ignored the sentiment and said, "I fell."

"No kidding." Another grunt, as aggrieved as his sigh, and he pushed to his feet. "Get out of there and find your own place for the night. This one's mine."

"There's no way out."

"Sure there is. It's called a door." He started walking away. Tess hurried over to the hole as he said, "Don't ask for my flashlight either. If you need light..."

He tossed something down. She caught a book of matches.

"Just don't burn the place down," he said. "You've done enough damage."

"You don't understand," she said. "There's no door."

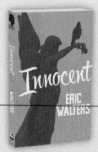